Melt My Heart, Cowboy

Melt My Heart, Cowboy

Cowboy

A Love at the Chocolate Shop Romance

C.J. Carmichael

TULE
PUBLISHING

Dedication

To Barbara Dunlop and Jane Porter and the 20th anniversary of our amazing friendship.

Acknowledgments

Thanks to all the talented and lovely authors who agreed to work with me on this project. I really landed the A-Team with Melissa McClone, Debra Salonen, Roxanne Snopek, Marin Thomas and Steena Holmes!

The idea for Love at the Chocolate Shop originated with my dear friend and publisher, Jane Porter. Thank you Jane, and all the wonderful Tule girls who worked so hard at concepts, cover design, editing, formatting and the million other tasks required to bring a series of twelve books into this world. My true gratitude to Meghan Farrell, Sinclair Sawhney, Lee Hyat, Lindsey Stover, Genevieve Cozart, and Monti Shalosky.

Chapter One

"CAN I TEMPT you with one of our cocoa peanut melts?" Rosie Linn wished she, herself, could tempt the good-looking cowboy on the other side of her sales counter.

But in the three months he'd been frequenting the Copper Mountain Chocolate shop—regular as Friday's happy hour at Grey's Saloon—he hadn't come close to asking her out. So she doubted that was going to happen.

Instead she pointed out one of the delicate and dreamy confections her boss, Sage Carrigan, had handcrafted just that morning. "Rich dark chocolate, swirled with creamy peanut goodness... what's not to love?"

The cowboy standing on the other side of the display case gave her a charming, slightly teasing smile, a smile that always made Rosie's day and often her entire week.

"I'm sure they're great, but I'll take the usual—a box of the dark chocolate salted caramels."

"Give these a taste, at least?" She proffered a tray with a sample of the cocoa peanut melts.

He just shook his head no. For months Rosie had been trying to entice him to try something other than a box of twelve Pink Himalayan Salted Chocolate Caramels.

But he would not be swayed.

"You don't know what you're missing."

The cowboy leaned an arm on the counter, and cocked an eyebrow. "I'm sure you're right, Rosie."

His use of her first name would have flattered her if it wasn't pinned to the front of her copper-colored apron.

"And if the chocolates were for me," he continued, "I'd be going on your recommendation for sure."

"But the chocolates aren't for you."

"Regretfully… no."

She waited, hoping he would tell her who they *were* for, but he said nothing further.

Rosie really wanted to know the name of the lucky recipient.

She had her speculations.

The most obvious, of course, was that he had a sweetheart with a chocolate addiction. This was not her favorite theory, however.

She far preferred the idea that he was a dutiful grandson, making a visit to an old folks' home.

But Sunday, not Friday, was the traditional time to visit the ill and the infirm.

Rosie knew this because, for the past five years, she'd nursed her diabetic father through a host of ailments until he'd finally succumbed to kidney failure. Most of the week she'd had to manage on her own, but on Sunday she could generally count on at least one or two neighbors or old friends to pop in with a casserole, or a vase of flowers.

With a pair of silver tongs, Rosie selected a dozen caramels bathed in rich, dark chocolate and speckled with pink Himalayan sea salt, sneaking glances at the cowboy as she carefully layered them into one of the shop's signature copper-colored boxes. She could tell by the dust on his boots, the worn leather of his belt, and the calluses on his hands, he was a working cowboy, not just someone dressing the part.

But that was pretty much all she knew about him.

"Anything else?" she asked.

"Still trying to tempt me, Rosie?" His gaze swept over *her*, not the display of chocolates.

"Is it working?"

"Oh, I'm plenty tempted, Rosie. Just doing my best to resist."

Her cheeks went hot as she wrapped the copper-colored box with some ribbon, wishing she could think of a clever retort. It was so frustrating that she excelled at writing clever dialogue for her brother's screenplays, yet so often found herself tongue-tied in real life.

Maybe if she could say just the right thing, he would ask her out. Of course, it would help her cause if she wasn't wearing her unbecoming work uniform.

The reddish-gold aprons looked fantastic on Sage, who had beautiful ginger hair and honey skin tones. But the hue did nothing for Rosie's ordinary brown hair and eyes. Probably she was beyond hope.

She slipped the box into a logo-embossed bag before handing it to the cowboy.

Her thanked her, but seemed in no hurry to leave. "Sure is quiet here today."

"It's been slow since the rodeo wrapped up. But last week was crazy." They'd sold all out of the chocolate molded cowboy hats that Sage created especially for the weekend long festivities.

"I'd hoped to watch the finals on Sunday. But the boss decided on Saturday we needed to start moving cattle."

"Is it big, the ranch where you work?"

"Yup."

She waited, hoping he would mention the ranch by name, but he didn't.

"Thanks, Rosie. Have yourself a nice weekend, now."

"Same to you."

The enticing possibility of something more in the future hung in the air for a few moments, as his gaze lingered. Then he gave her a parting nod and left.

Outside, he stopped under the front awning.

Wherever he was headed, he didn't seem in a hurry to get there.

Rosie leaned against the counter, watching as he settled

his hat over his dark, curly hair, and then squared his shoulders. For a moment she thought he might turn on his heels and come back inside. But five seconds later, he was on his way.

Which meant she wouldn't see him again for another week.

She sighed, not sure why, in a town that specialized in hot masculine dating material, it was this particular cowboy who'd caught her eye.

Maybe it was the hint of sadness she sometimes glimpsed in his eyes that intrigued her. Or it might be because of the time she'd seen him make funny faces at a crying baby, whose mother was trying to pick out a gift for her mother-in-law. The fussing baby had grown silent as he stared at the cowboy's silly expressions. Then he'd smiled, and finally he'd chortled adorably.

The cowboy had brushed off the mother's thanks, winking at Rosie before leaving the shop with his usual box of chocolate salted caramels.

A cowboy who was good with babies. What woman wouldn't love that?

Rosie sure had. But he hadn't asked her out then, or in any of the weeks that followed and it was probably for the best because Rosie had plans and they didn't include Marietta.

As soon as the old family house was sold she was going to move to L.A. and live with her screenwriter, older brother,

Daniel, and his actress wife, Glenda. Over the past few years she'd been helping Daniel with some of his scripts. She'd started out proofreading, then had begun making the odd suggestion.

Lately she'd progressed to entire scenes and at their father's funeral Daniel had invited her to work with him full-time, with the credit and pay to go with it.

He'd already had a few minor successes with some low budget, made-for-TV movies. Now he—well, both of them actually—were working on a TV series for a major network. Daniel was hoping this would catapult his career—*their* careers—to the next level. Rosie prayed he was right.

She loved this town and working at the chocolate shop. And she'd never regret spending these last years with her father.

But she was tired of getting all her excitement vicariously—from books, movies, and Daniel's accounts of the parties and night life he and Glenda enjoyed. She wanted to be part of the action.

If only the darn house would sell. It had been on the market now for over six months without so much as a hint of an offer. The leaves that had been a fresh new green at her father's funeral now sparkled butterscotch yellow in the autumn sun. October already.

Rosie sighed, then turned to look down Main Street. The local merchants had already replaced the rustic fence posts, bales of hay, and posters advertising the Copper Mountain

Rodeo with spooky Halloween ghosts, witches, and zombies in preparation for the next major holiday. Just last night Sage had decorated the chocolate shop's window with fat, orange pumpkins and some matching Halloween inspired products.

Time was passing all too quickly.

Rosie made a promise to herself. She would be gone before the first snowfall. She couldn't take another long, cold Montana winter.

ROSIE WAS ABOUT to start closing up the shop for the night when a pretty woman, definitely under thirty, came through the door, rolling a large suitcase behind her.

"Hi! Is Sage Carrigan here?"

The woman had almond-colored eyes, creamy skin, and a lovely smile. She wasn't tall, but she had a curvy figure, shown to perfection in her outfit of jeans, fashion boots, and a chunky wool sweater.

Not in a million years could Rosie have put together an outfit that looked so flattering and casually chic.

"Sage isn't here right now. May I help you?"

The woman's face fell and suddenly she looked younger than Rosie had first guessed. Early twenties, max, just a few years younger than Rosie herself.

"Thanks, but I really need to talk to Sage. She's my aunt."

Rosie knew Sage had three sisters. The youngest, Callan,

was married without children and still lived and operated the family's ranch, the Circle C. The next in line was Dani, who lived in Seattle with her husband and a daughter and new-born baby boy.

Which meant this girl must belong to Mattie, the oldest of the Carrigan sisters. Mattie and her second-husband had a ranch somewhere in the Flathead Valley.

"Are you one of Mattie's twins?"

She blinked with surprise. "I'm Portia. How did you guess?"

"It's a small town and I've been working for Sage since she opened her shop." She'd been here when Sage's ex, Dawson O'Dell, had shown up in town with his young daughter, Savannah, intent on winning back Sage's heart. Now they were married and had added a cute baby boy to the family. Again, Rosie was reminded of how quickly the years were passing.

"I'm Rosie Linn by the way."

"Nice to meet you."

As Rosie stepped out from behind the counter to shake her hand, she noticed Portia's gaze sweep down from her apron to her less-than-stylish black pants and the clogs she wore to work because they were so comfortable.

"Great outfit, huh? Sage insists we wear these copper-colored aprons. Dakota—she works here part-time as well—hates them, too."

Portia rolled her eyes sympathetically. "I once worked in

a restaurant where I had to wear this t-shirt with a picture of a chicken. It was pathetic. Still, the apron isn't bad, it's just too dull against the black shirt and trousers. If it were up to me, I'd pair it with a cobalt blue shirt and some really dark, crisp blue jeans."

"Yeah?" Rosie made a mental note to do some online shopping later that evening.

"So, about my aunt, do you have any idea where I could find her?"

"She would have picked Savannah up from school at three-thirty. So they're probably home by now."

Portia wrinkled her nose. "I was hoping to talk to her here, rather than at her house. I thought it might be… easier." As she spoke, she pulled out her phone. "I'll send her a text."

When she was finished, Portia wheeled her suitcase into a corner then strolled around the shop, pausing here and there to make minor adjustments to the stock. In every case, she managed to somehow make the displays look better. Rosie was impressed. This girl had a good eye. Rosie wondered if maybe she could get more fashion tips from Portia. She didn't want to look like a country hick when she finally made her move to L.A.

"How is business?" Portia asked.

"This week has been slow. But rodeo week was terrific. And summer was quite good as well."

"And with the holidays coming… Halloween, Thanksgiving, Christmas… the trend should continue upward, right?"

"November and December are two of our busier months, that's true." Rosie glanced from Portia to the big suitcase.

Before she could say anything more Portia came round the counter and put a hand on her arm.

"I might as well tell you what's going on, Rosie. I've just dropped out of college and I'm hoping my Aunt Sage will give me a job. Do you think I have a chance?"

"I don't know." Seeing the worry in Portia's eyes, Rosie instinctively wanted to give her hope. "Chances are pretty good actually, since I'm going to be leaving soon."

"You are?"

"My dad passed away this spring. He was my last tie to this town. As soon as our house sells, I'm moving to L.A. Sage knows this, it's not a secret or anything." And then, before she could stop herself, she asked, "Why did you drop out of college?"

Portia turned away, wrapping her arms around her body. "Sorry to hear about your father. That's rough. As for college, I was only going to please my mother. I decided it was time I stopped wasting her money and my time."

Sounded logical. But Rosie knew how emotional parents could get about higher education. Her own father had argued for months when she'd told him she was turning down her scholarship to stay home and look after him.

"What were you taking?"

"Just arts."

"How far along?"

Again Portia looked away. "Senior year."

Rosie bit back the obvious question. Why not finish after going so far? But Portia, who was so friendly in most respects, clearly wasn't open to further discussion on this topic. She moved to the far end of the shop and then pulled out her phone again and began scrolling.

"My aunt's coming to pick me up." She announced a minute later. "Mind if I hang out until she gets here?"

"No problem. Want a cup of hot cocoa while you're waiting?"

"Oh, I'd love that. Aunt Sage sends me chocolates all the time, but I've never tasted her cocoa."

"It's to die for." Rosie turned to the back counter, where a copper pot rested on the built-in gas range top. She raised the heat and then used a wooden spoon to stir the molten chocolate concoction.

Lured by the aroma, Portia moved closer again.

"Oh, my God, that looks so decadent. What's in it?"

"It's your aunt's secret recipe. But I know she uses pure chocolate, lots of cream, and a dash of cinnamon. Would you like whipped cream and chocolate shavings on top?"

"Not normally. But after all those hours on the bus, I'd say I deserve a treat. Sure, go for it."

Once the cocoa was steaming, Rosie ladled a serving into a tall mug, then added a spoonful of thick, sweet cream, and a generous shaking of dark chocolate shavings.

One sip had Portia moaning. "I can't believe I've never tried this until now."

Rosie smiled. She loved witnessing someone tasting Sage's hot cocoa for the first time.

Portia savored a few more mouthfuls, then nodded at the copper pot. "Why don't you have some too, then sit and talk with me for a while."

They hadn't had a customer since Portia arrived, so Rosie saw no reason not to agree, but first she slipped the pages of the screenplay she'd been working on during the lulls in business into her large purse.

She only worked on her stories when there was absolutely nothing left for her to do in the shop, but she still felt guilty about it. Besides, no one but family knew she helped Daniel with his screenplays.

She and Portia sat at one of the small tables at the rear of the shop, next to the door to the kitchen. Sage had added this small sitting area a few years ago when it became clear that some visitors wanted to linger and enjoy their cocoa inside—especially during the winter months.

It had proven so popular Sage had begun to consider expanding her square footage. But so far she hadn't taken any action on the plan.

"So, Rosie," Portia said, "tell me about yourself."

Rosie swirled her spoon through the whipped cream and cocoa. "Not much to say. I'm probably the most boring person in Marietta."

"I don't believe that."

"I've lived here all my life. Only had one job and that's this one."

"What about guys? Do you have a boyfriend?"

"No one serious. To be honest, I haven't dated anyone in at least six months."

Portia's eyes rounded. No doubt she would consider a *month* to be an intolerable dry spell.

"I'm in a rut, and not a good one," Rosie admitted. "When I was in high school, my father began suffering from serious complications from his diabetes. Against his protests, I put off going to college so he wouldn't have to go into a care home."

"You must have been really close."

"It's been just the two of us for a long time. My brother is twelve years older. I can hardly remember when he lived at home. And my mom died from cancer several years ago."

"I'm sorry."

"Dad took her death especially hard. He used to write bestselling thrillers, but after Mom died he never wrote again."

"How tragic."

"Yes. It's been tough."

"I can see why you want to move. What are your plans when you get to L.A.?"

Rosie told her about Daniel and his wife. "They've

promised to find me a job of some sort," she finished vaguely, not wanting to reveal her writing aspirations. "I'm willing to try anything to get out of this town."

"Not that Marietta is a bad place," Rosie added quickly. "I just need a change."

"I know that feeling,"

Rosie raised her eyebrows inquiringly.

Portia seemed on the verge of elaborating, but then the door opened and Sage rushed in. Even with her hair in a messy updo, and wearing yoga gear with a toddler perched on her hip, Sage looked gorgeous.

Rosie immediately leapt to her feet, worried her boss would think she'd been lazing around. While Sage was one of the sweetest people Rosie knew, she had exacting standards when it came to her chocolate shop.

But Sage wasn't even looking at Rosie.

"Portia what's going on? Shouldn't you be at college in Seattle?"

And suddenly, shockingly, Portia started to cry.

Chapter Two

THIS TOWN SURE is full of pretty women. As Brant Willington passed a sweet, young thing, lugging a big suitcase along Main Street, his thoughts were still on the chocolate shop sales clerk. The fifteen minutes he spent chatting with Rosie and resisting her attempts to get him to buy something new were the highlight of his Friday afternoons. If he was in a different place in his life, he'd be tempted to ask her out.

But he had no time for dating. Between his job and his obligations to Sara Maria he was pretty much tapped out.

Thinking of the evening ahead, his stomach felt the way it had as a kid when he'd been in the waiting room for the dentist. The antiseptic smell, the whining of the drill, those things had made him want to bolt.

Which was what he longed to do right now.

If this had been a regular Friday night three months earlier, he would be in the bar with his buddies right now, looking forward to a few games of pool and possibly a little dancing and romancing, if he found the right girl.

But those days were gone now. Probably forever.

Brant forced his feet to move in the direction of the May Bell Care Home. The small town was quiet in the aftermath of the rodeo, but with the aspen leaves newly golden, he'd never seen it look prettier. Longingly he glanced down the block to Grey's Saloon, before turning on Second, then again on Church.

And there it was.

From the outside it looked pleasant enough. A three story brick building with nice landscaping out front, including two benches, which were both currently occupied.

He nodded at an older lady settled on the bench to his left, with her hands resting on her walker.

"Good afternoon, Mrs. Powell."

"Hello, Brant. It's nice to see you. Your visits are the highlight of her week you know."

Mrs. Powell was so arthritic she could hardly walk, but mentally she was a force to be reckoned with. Brant considered it both a blessing and a curse that she had the room next to Sara Maria's.

Inside, he stopped briefly to check-in at reception, before turning right and walking to the end of the hall. The door to Sara Maria's room was shut, which meant she was still watching *Jeopardy*.

Brant squared his shoulders. Sara Maria had been born ten years after him. He'd adored his cute baby sister at first, and the feeling had been mutual. His mom had always said that when Brant was in the room Sara Maria would look at no one else.

Then Sara Maria turned two. And all of a sudden she'd changed. She'd become quiet and withdrawn. No more smiles, no more adoring gazes at her brother. After numerous doctors' appointments and hours of scouring the internet, his mother had come to realize Sara Maria was autistic.

Family life had never been the same after that, especially once their father left. Their mother had borne the brunt of the burden, until three months ago, when she'd been killed in a car crash.

Now Brant was the head of the family. If only he had half the strength and patience of his mother.

Brant inhaled deeply, then tapped on the door and walked into the darkened room. Sara Maria had closed the curtains to eliminate any glare on the TV screen. She was sitting in her chair, gaze fixed on her favorite show. She didn't even glance at him as he crossed in front of her to perch on the edge of her neatly made bed.

On screen the show host gave the name of a city.

"What is the capital of Belize," Sara Maria responded quickly, before any of the contestants.

"How the hell did you know that?" Brant shook his head in amazement.

She didn't have the good judgement to turn off the stove burner after using it, yet she knew facts about the world he had no clue about.

Predictably Sara Maria ignored his praise. When she was watching television or a movie, she devoted one-hundred percent of her concentration to it.

Five minutes later, after the show had ended, Brant knew enough to let all the credits roll and wait for a commercial to start playing before turning off the TV. To do otherwise, to shorten her program by so much as one second, could cause a tantrum.

The moment the room was silent, Sara Maria finally looked at him. "Did you bring me my chocolates?"

He resisted the urge to tease her by pretending he'd forgotten. Such pranks never ended well.

"Sure did." He handed her the bag.

"Thank you, Brant."

"No problem." He went to the window and pushed open the curtains, so he could stare out at the view while she ate the first of her treats. He didn't need to watch to know she would first lick the pink flecks of salt from the top, then the chocolate coating on each side of the square until all that was left was the caramel, at which point she would finally pop the damn thing in her mouth.

He'd had sixteen years to get used to his sister's peculiarities and her obsession with routine. But not until three months ago had he realized how much his mother had acted as a buffer between the two of them.

Mom had filled the awkward silences with cheerful chatter. She'd protected Sara Maria, while giving her son the freedom he'd craved.

Only now did Brant wonder if she'd felt as trapped as he did.

"I'm finished. Can we go for pizza now?"

"Maybe we should try the Main Street Diner for a change," he teased.

She didn't even smile. She almost never did.

"Friday is pizza night."

Her total lack of a sense of humor was tough to deal with. He remembered complaining to his mom, who had cautioned him not to judge. "You're not so normal yourself, Brant. Who grows up to be a cowboy in this day and age?"

Touché, Mom.

"Yup, let's go for pizza." He handed his sister her jacket, careful to not touch her fingers. Sara Maria hated physical contact.

The Pizza Parlor was on Front Street, conveniently located less than a block from the movie theater where they'd be going next. Their walk was a silent one. If Sara Maria had any thoughts, she didn't share them, and neither did Brant share his, which had circled back to the curly-haired clerk at the chocolate shop, with the sweet, round face. He wondered what she was doing this evening. Probably something a heck of a lot more interesting than he was.

The silence between him and his sister continued after they'd been seated in a booth and handed menus they wouldn't need because they always ordered the same thing.

Several years ago, his sister had turned vegetarian after watching an upsetting documentary on the meat processing industry. Even their mother's attempts to source "happy" chickens and "free range" beef hadn't swayed Sara Maria, and eventually all their family meals became vegetarian because she wouldn't touch her food if there was any sort of meat product on the table.

As they waited for their veggie pizza and colas to arrive, Brant glanced around at the other diners. There were several families as well as couples out on a date night. He glanced longingly at a table of guys who looked to be in their late twenties like him. He'd bet their biggest worry right now was whether they'd be able to talk any ladies into dancing with them later tonight at Grey's.

As Brant was watching, one of the guys at the table noticed Sara Maria. He sat up tall, the way a guy would do when he spotted a pretty woman. But after a few seconds the guy's admiring smile was replaced by a puzzled shrug.

It was a familiar reaction.

Brant's sister was very pretty, with light blonde hair and delicately feminine features.

It was only on the second glance, or possibly the third, that someone picked up the "different" vibe. And that was obviously what the guy at the other table was sensing.

Brant looked for their server, anxious for the food to arrive so he'd have something to focus on besides his sister's quiet presence. He took a sip of water, then adjusted his place setting.

"Stop playing with your cutlery," Sara Maria said, mirroring the very words his mother had often spoken to him.

Brant let out a breath of relief as he spied the server coming with their order.

He'd only finished his first slice, when Sara Maria said, "Mom is in heaven."

Brant's stomach tightened, and his appetite ebbed. "Yup."

"She's never coming back."

"No." He reached for his cola.

Why did she insist on saying these things every, single time he saw her? He got that she couldn't help her various eccentricities. But why did talking about their mother's death have to be one of them?

Aware his sister was still looking at him, Brant gulped the rest of his cola, then pulled out his wallet.

"I'm not finished eating."

"No rush," he lied.

It wasn't until twenty minutes later, when they were seated in the theater watching previews for upcoming movies that Brant could finally relax. This was the only time he truly enjoyed being with his sister, mostly because he could sort of forget about her. As long as he bought her a small box of popcorn and a bottle of water, as long as the movie wasn't overly sexual or violent, he could count on her being still and quiet until the credits finished rolling.

And, yes, they had to stay until the screen had gone dark before they could finally leave.

But Brant didn't mind that part, just as the walk back to the care home would be fine as well. His sister liked to analyze movies after she'd seen them, and she did just as good a job as any film critic he'd ever seen on television. Generally, she would talk without the need for any response from him about the film for the entire walk home, at which point he could hand her over to the care of the evening nurse with a clear conscience.

After all, he'd done his duty.

And he'd have an entire week to himself, before he had to do it all over again.

Only this night didn't go according to plan.

The night nurse at the care home was waiting for him when they walked in the main doors. Donna was a short woman, with stocky legs and tight blonde curls, about mid-thirties. While she had a quick and easy smile, her eyes always seemed to be quietly judging him.

Or that was how she made him feel, anyway.

"Hi, Sara Maria. Did you have a nice night out with your brother?"

"The movie was rated seventy-four on Rotten Tomatoes. I think it should have been seventy-eight, at least."

"Is that so?" She turned to Brant. "Before you leave, could I have a quick word?"

"Sure," he said, feeling ambushed.

Leaving Sara Maria to head to her room and prepare for bed, the nurse led Brant to the first floor lounge room, where they both sat down.

"Brant, Margie from admin has been trying to reach you."

He nodded, guiltily aware of not having returned any of her messages.

"You can't keep avoiding her, Brant. Or the fact that your sister no longer fits in here with us at the care home."

Oh, God. He so did not want to hear this.

"When you first brought her to us in July, she was hardly eating, and wouldn't communicate with anyone."

He nodded. His sister had taken their mother's death badly, in fact had suffered a total breakdown. She'd been hospitalized for several weeks before she'd finally improved to a state where he could move her here.

"At that point, she was a good candidate for us. But this last month she's made remarkable strides. Emotionally, she's on an even keel. And she manages all of her daily needs completely independently."

Brant studied the nurse's eyes, trying to figure out if he could appeal to her sympathy. "Yeah, but she's still not capable of living on her own."

"Is there another family member she could move in with?"

He thought of his dad, who'd been out of their lives since Sara Maria's autism diagnosis. Remarried with two young children, their father made it clear he was good for the occasional visit and regular financial contributions to Sara Maria's care and nothing else.

"Not really."

She shook her head, looking genuinely worried. "I'm not sure what to suggest then. Maybe you could explore other living arrangements for the two of you?"

He crossed his arms over his chest. "I work on a ranch outside of Bozeman and live in a bunkhouse with three other guys."

"I see. Well, that is tricky."

"I brought Sara Maria here on the understanding this would be a long-term arrangement. My sister likes routine. She'd be upset if I moved her."

"We're not going to kick her out, if that's what you're afraid of. But you need to think about what's best for your sister. She's bored here, I'm afraid. Her potential—which is much greater than we initially accessed—is terribly underutilized."

Brant stared at the woman as if she'd just handed him a prison sentence.

But it wasn't Nurse Donna's fault. His fate had been imposed the moment after his mother died.

His sister's welfare was in his hands and it would remain that way for the rest of his life.

No chance of parole.

Chapter Three

S AGE WAS HANDING Portia a copper apron when Rosie
arrived for work on Saturday morning.

"Good morning, Rosie," Sage said. "I'm glad you're here.
You can show Portia how to ring in sales and explain how
our pricing works. I've just outlined the shop rules concern-
ing dress and cleanliness."

Sage sounded distracted, which meant her mind was on
something else… no doubt she had some chocolates at a
delicate stage of production.

"I guess you got the job." Rosie smiled at Portia. "Congratulations."

Portia and Sage exchanged a glance loaded with emotion.
Rosie imagined they'd had a long discussion last night. No
doubt Sage had tried to talk her niece into finishing her
degree, but obviously she hadn't succeeded.

"Portia will be working rotating hours, some days with
you, others with Dakota," Sage said. "She's also agreed to
handle some of our marketing duties, like maintaining the
website and organizing special events."

"That's great." Sage was awesome at creating delicious chocolate treats, but in Rosie's view she didn't spend nearly as much effort on promotion as she should.

Besides, it would be fun to have someone new to work with. After just a few hours, Portia proved to be a quick learner. Business was a bit more brisk now that it was the weekend, but between customers they chatted about music, fashion, and their mutual love for quirky rom-coms.

Several times Rosie was tempted to tell Portia about the TV pilot she and Daniel were working on. It had some elements that reminded her of the *Gilmore Girls*, but with more action and a thread of mystery running throughout. She just knew Portia would love it.

But talking about the pilot would mean coming clean about her part in the writing. And it was too soon for that.

At lunch time, Sage came out of the kitchen looking pleased. "My dark chocolate truffles turned out perfectly. Why don't the two of you take your lunch break together? I'll watch the shop until you're back."

Happy for the rare opportunity to go out for lunch— normally she ate a sandwich and apple from home—Rosie whipped her apron over her head.

"I need to use the restroom first," Portia said. "Meet you out front in a few minutes?"

"Sure." Rosie was going to sit on the outside bench and soak up some sunshine, but Sage stopped her.

"Could I have a quick word, Rosie?"

Her mouth went dry. Surely Sage wasn't going to fire her to make room for her niece? Though she was planning to leave, eventually, Rosie had hoped to work as long as she was still living in Marietta.

Slowly she turned to face her boss.

"Though you've never asked, I've sensed you wouldn't have minded working some extra hours each week, Rosie. And now that I've hired Portia, I'm not going to be able to give them to you, at least for a while."

"That's okay." Rosie smiled with relief. "I'm still planning to move to L.A. once the house sells."

"Have you had any offers?"

"Not yet." She couldn't blame her realtor Maddie Cash.

Maddie had brought in lots of prospective buyers, but so far none of them had been able to see beyond the rotting porch and peeling paint on the home's exterior. It went against the grain to hire someone other than Edmond Burgess to do the work—for as long as Rosie could remember her father had hired him for all their family's painting and home repairs—but since Edmond always seemed to be too busy, perhaps she ought to find someone else.

"Well, I'm sure going to be sorry to lose you when you go. In the meantime I'm glad you don't have a problem with my niece working here."

"I think it's great," Rosie assured her.

"Good." Sage hesitated, then added, "I'm afraid Portia's in a fragile place right now. She told you she dropped out of her senior year at the University of Washington?"

Rosie nodded.

"Something must have happened to make her take such a drastic step. I don't know what. She refuses to talk about it. But she needs a safe place to hide from the world right now."

And what safer place than working in a chocolate shop in Marietta, Montana?

"I'm glad you gave her the job. I think it will be fun to work with her."

Sage's smile showed her relief. "I was hoping you two would get along. Maybe you can introduce Portia to some of your friends. Show her around town and help her feel at home."

"I'd be happy to do that." Not that she had many friends to introduce.

Her best friends in high school had mostly moved away for college, careers, or to follow other dreams, and she'd drifted apart from the rest. Rosie supposed to most people her age she was deadly dull, but going out to drink and party when her father was alone and sick at home had never felt right.

Portia emerged from the washroom then, looking pale, but smiling. "So where should we go for lunch?"

The day was gloriously sunny. Rosie felt almost giddy with the prospect of an hour of unexpected free time. "Beck's is known for amazing bison burgers."

"Hm. A little heavy for lunch."

Rosie guessed Portia would feel the same about her second choice, pizza. "They have nice salads at the Main Street Diner."

Portia brightened. "That sounds perfect. I hope it isn't too far?"

"Are you kidding? You know you're in Marietta, right?"

Portia laughed. "It's funny. I've spent a lot of holidays visiting my mom's family, but we mostly stay on the Circle C Ranch. The few times we go to town, it's usually to watch the rodeo."

"Trust me, it won't take long until you know our downtown better than your own home."

"Don't be so sure. I swear I'm directionally challenged."

"Well, in Marietta, all you have to do is turn in the direction of Copper Mountain to orient yourself. The mountain and the court house are both due west. And the Main Street Diner we're going to for lunch is right across from the court house, just two blocks away."

"Sounds simple. I remember getting so lost in Seattle after my first frat party. Of course all the beer I'd been drinking didn't help."

Rosie felt a twinge of envy. As they walked the two blocks to the diner, she asked Portia for more details about college life.

"I partied way too much my first semester," Portia admitted. "Then I met this really great guy—he helped me get my head on straight."

"Are you still seeing him?"

"No." Portia stopped smiling and fell silent, reminding Rosie of how she'd reacted yesterday when she'd been questioned about dropping out of college.

Was this great guy she'd mentioned connected to her decision to quit?

ONCE THEY'D BEEN seated at the diner, Portia quickly became cheerful again, and the two of them talked nonstop over their lunch. Portia half-complained and half-bragged about her brainy twin sister, Wren, who was studying geology at the University of Colorado in Boulder. In turn, Rosie shared about her brother Daniel and some of the interesting people he'd worked with so far in his career.

"That's so cool that he's actually had two screenplays turned into movies. Have I heard of them?"

"They were both made-for-TV movies. His wife, Glenda, was the female lead for the second one. That's how they met."

"Oh, how romantic. I love it. Do you visit them very often? Have you been on a movie set when they're filming?"

Rosie sighed. "Daniel and Glenda have invited me. But it was difficult to travel while our father was alive. He couldn't be left alone for more than a day." Portia didn't ask for details, and Rosie didn't offer them.

She'd learned discussions about insulin injections and

other medical minutia were not interesting conversational fodder for the majority of people unless they happened to be a doctor or a nurse.

"So, you've never even been to L.A?"

"No."

"Maybe you should check it out before you move there. What if you don't like it?"

"Seriously? Of course I'll love it. It won't be Marietta, that's the main thing."

"It must be an expensive place to live, though?"

"My brother's house has a separate casita with a bedroom, kitchenette, and bathroom. They're going to let me stay rent-free for the first few months. It's right by the outdoor pool. The whole place looks like a spread in a decorating magazine."

"I'm sure it's beautiful. It's just—sometimes you don't realize how much you miss home until you leave."

Rosie ate the last leaf of kale from her plate. Portia had barely touched her own lunch. All she'd had so far was a piece of sourdough bread and a glass of water.

"Were you homesick in college?"

"I had lots of fun. But I did miss home. Unfortunately for me, there's no going back. My parents split up during my freshman year. Now my mom is married to someone else and lives at his place. Nat is a great guy and his house is incredible—but when I go to stay with them, it doesn't feel like home."

31

"I know what you mean. My house feels so empty now that it's just me and Huck."

Portia's eyes widened. "Huck? Have you been holding out on me?"

Rosie laughed. "He's my father's golden lab. The poor guy is so depressed, he misses Dad terribly. I'm hoping whoever buys the house will be willing to take Huck on, as well. He sure wouldn't do well in L.A."

Not only that, but Rosie was pretty sure neither Daniel nor Glenda would want him.

"Any other fellas you haven't told me about?" Portia teased.

Rosie hesitated. "It's kind of silly—but there is this cowboy who comes into the store every Friday afternoon to buy chocolates. In fact, he'd just stopped in a few minutes before you yesterday."

"I think I know the one. I passed by this really good-looking guy on the street. I noticed he was carrying a Copper Mountain Chocolate shop bag. He was a real hottie."

"Right?"

"What's his name?"

"I don't know! I know nothing about him, at all. We always chat when he comes into the shop—and he does flirt a little. But whenever I try to find out anything about him, he shuts right down."

"Ah—a man of mystery. How intriguing."

"I'd love to know who he buys the chocolates for. I don't

think they're for him. And somehow I don't feel they're for a girlfriend, either. At least I hope not."

AFTER HIS VISIT with his sister, Brant generally headed home to the bunkhouse at the Three Bars Ranch. If his buddies were back from the bar, they'd play a bit of poker, drink a few beers. All of them were about the same age—late twenties to early thirties—and they were friends as well as coworkers.

This Friday, however, he'd splurged on a night at the historic Graff Hotel on Front Avenue, Marietta. After breakfast he'd gone back to the care home and spoken to Margie in admin as well as another nurse, Nadia Jackson. Both women had relayed the same message.

Sara Maria was bored and lonely. The care home was no longer the right place for her.

After those unsettling conversations, Brant decided to take a walk. He always thought better when he was active and this morning he had a lot to mull over. At least the day was a beauty, the sort Montana was famous for. Enjoying the sunshine and warm air, Brant headed over the bridge to the fair grounds.

A person could hardly tell there'd been a rodeo here last week. Every last bit of trash had been removed and the ground in the rodeo arena was clean and raked. Brant walked by all the loading chutes, past the grandstands and the concession buildings until he came to River Bend Park.

Copper Mountain stood to his right now, the peak dusted with a light snowfall from the previous night. A sign winter was coming.

Good thing they'd moved the cattle down to the lower pastures last week. The boss might be right in his hunch winter was coming early this year.

Brant ambled past the library, following a pathway that skirted a row of beautiful homes on Bramble Lane.

He wished he had someone to talk his situation over with. His buddies at the Three Bars wouldn't get it. None of them had so much as a serious girlfriend to worry about.

There was his father. But Ted's reaction to any problem involving Sara Maria was to offer more money, and lack of cash wasn't the problem here.

Their father had already set Sara Maria up with a generous trust fund, and that had been supplemented by insurance proceeds after their mother's death. But money couldn't keep a person from getting lonely.

Brant was back on Main Street when he noticed two women on the other side of the street, about a block ahead of him. They were so engrossed in their conversation they seemed unaware of anyone else, certainly not him. But he remembered them both. The shorter one had been pulling a suitcase on Main Street yesterday. The tall one with the crazy, curly hair was Rosie.

He couldn't help but smile and his first impulse was to

head toward them, maybe chat a little with Rosie.

Then another idea occurred to him. Rosie couldn't be more than twenty-four, twenty-five—not that much older than Sara Maria. She and her friend would be a heck of a lot more interesting to his sister than the folks in the care home. Maybe he could hire one of them to spend time with his sister?

Even as he was thinking all this, the young women were turning into the chocolate shop. Without pausing to second-guess the impulse, he loped down the block, crossed the street, and followed them inside.

They were putting on their aprons, and still chatting, when he opened the door, but by the time he'd stepped over the threshold they fell silent. He was reminded of the way a classroom would suddenly become dead quiet when the teacher walked in.

"Hey." He nodded at Rosie first, then at her friend. "I was wondering if you could help me with something."

"Changed your mind about the cocoa peanut melts?"

He grinned. "No. But thanks, anyway. The thing is, I'm not from around here so I don't know many locals. But I need to hire someone for some part-time help."

"What sort of help?" Portia wondered.

"It's complicated. Maybe one of you could join me for a coffee. Give me a chance to pick your brains?"

Portia raised her eyebrows. "Are you sure it's our *brains* you want to pick?"

He put his right hand to his chest. "I promise my intentions are legit. My name is Brant Willington. I work at the Three Bars Ranch west of Bozeman."

"I'm Portia Bishop and this is Rosie Linn."

"Oh, I know Rosie." He glanced from Portia to the girl who was always trying to tempt him to try something new. "So, what do you say about that cup of coffee?" Though he'd issued his invitation to both of them, he hoped Rosie would be the one to say yes.

Unwittingly, Portia helped his cause by shrugging her shoulders. "I'm new to town as well. But Rosie's lived in Marietta all her life. She's the perfect person for you to talk with."

"Great." He glanced again at Rosie, who looked a bit flustered. He hoped he hadn't put her on the spot. "Is this a good time?"

Before Rosie could answer, her friend stepped over and swept Rosie's apron over her head. "It sure is. We'll be lucky if we get two customers in the next thirty minutes. I'll be fine on my own."

"I see there's a coffee place across the street. What do you say Rosie?"

Chapter Four

THE INTOXICATING AROMA of coffee and the chattering of a half-dozen different conversations helped Rosie relax as she stepped inside the Java Café. Brant had held the door open for her. The last date she'd gone out with hadn't done that. Of course the last date had been months ago, set up by the lawyer who'd handled her father's estate, so she might be remembering incorrectly.

And, of course, this wasn't a date.

Brant asked what she wanted, then suggested she sit at a table for two by the window, while he lined up to get their drinks.

Rosie noticed the cute woman behind the counter flirt as Brant place their order. He seemed oblivious. She supposed he was used to that sort of reaction from women, and she blushed to think of how desperately she'd tried to impress him for the past three months.

Yet now, suddenly, she was here, about to have coffee with him.

What sort of part-time worker was he looking for? If it

meant spending time with him, she was all for it.

"Here's your skinny latte. Did you want any sugar?"

"No thanks, this is perfect." She noticed he'd ordered black coffee. She kind of liked that in a guy.

"So, you've lived in Marietta all your life?"

"That's right. How about you?"

"I was born in Chicago. But my parents split when I was thirteen and, at that point, my mother moved us to be near her folks in Bozeman. So I've called Montana home more than half my life."

He gestured occasionally when he was talking and she noticed that while his skin was working-man tough, his fingers were long and slender. On another man they would have looked elegant, but this guy was every inch cowboy.

"You said you work on a ranch. Do you like it?"

"Hell, yeah. More fun than working with chocolate all day I'd wager."

She smiled. "That's a bet I'd be willing to take. Working at Copper Mountain Chocolates is pretty awesome."

"So is being on the back of a loyal horse on a sunny autumn day."

"I bet your job isn't quite as much fun when our January blizzards hit."

"True. But every job has a downside."

"Not mine." Except, maybe, the copper-colored aprons.

"It must take a lot of willpower though, to stay slim when you're surrounded by all those delicious chocolates."

"I made a pact with myself when I started working with Sage. I decided I would only have one treat each day. It might be a cup of cocoa one day, or a single truffle the next. But I always limit myself to just one thing."

"Seriously? You don't ever cheat?"

"Nope." She'd seen what unhealthy eating had done for her father, cutting off his lifespan by at least a decade. "Anytime I get a craving I just remind myself that I can have it the next day."

"You'd get a kick out of my sister. I buy her a box of chocolates every Friday and she always makes them last an entire week."

"So that's who you buy those chocolates for! I couldn't help but wonder, with you being such a regular customer."

"Yeah, they're for my younger sister, Sara Maria. She's why I wanted to talk to you. She just turned eighteen and she's autistic."

Rosie sat back. This was one possibility she simply hadn't imagined. "Like the Sheldon character on *Big Bang Theory?*"

"Sheldon's character is portrayed as pretty high-functioning, but quirky. My sister... well, she has her quirks, all right. But she lives in her own world most of the time. It can be hard to reach her."

He started drumming his fingers on the table top. Rosie could feel his anxiety level rising.

"So where does Sara Maria live?"

"Used to be with my mom, in one of the apartments on

Church Street. But Mom died in a car crash this summer."

"I'm so sorry."

"Thanks." He glanced down for a second, composing himself. "Sara Maria took the news badly. She had a sort of breakdown and had to be hospitalized. Since then she's been living in the May Bell Care Home."

"I know the place. As care homes go, it's very nice." Still, she was glad she'd never had to place her father in it. Leaving the home he and Mom had moved into as newlyweds would have broken his heart, and hers, too.

"It took her a while to adjust. But the nurses think now that she's recovering from her grief, she's getting bored and well... lonely. She needs to hang out with people closer to her own age. That's why I want to hire someone."

"So this is where I come in." Rosie sank back into her seat, disappointed despite herself. She wouldn't be spending time with him, but with his sister. Filling the caregiver role again, just as she'd done with her parents. Wasn't that just her luck?

"You're a few years old than her, but I was hoping you could take her out for hikes, maybe. Or go shopping. Whatever girls that age like to do."

"I could probably get you a list of names. Nice people. I'm sure they'd be very caring toward your sister."

"I was thinking...that is..." He scratched the side of his neck looking uncomfortable before adding, "What about you? I'd pay you whatever you make at the chocolate shop."

Seeing the prospect of rejection in her eyes, he amended his offer. "Plus an additional ten percent."

Rosie stared at him blankly. He had no idea, of course, that she'd spent the past six years of her life as a caregiver for her father. Phase two of her life was supposed to involve writing screenplays for Hollywood. Pedicures and cocktail parties. Floating in her brother's darling, outdoor swimming pool.

"The problem is I'm planning to move soon. To L.A."

His eyes rounded. "Marietta to L.A. That's drastic."

"I need drastic. I've lived in this town my entire life. I stayed for my father, but he passed away this spring. As soon as I sell our house I'm going to be out of here. I'd hate to take your job only to leave you in the lurch a few months down the road."

Even as she gave the excuse she felt dishonest. If the job had involved spending time with him instead of his autistic sister, she wouldn't have let a potential move to L.A. stop her from saying yes.

"A few months would be a big help. It would give me time to find someone more permanent."

Man, this guy was not giving her a graceful out.

"I have no experience with people like your sister."

"Would you be willing to meet her, at least? See if the two of you like each other?"

It wasn't fair that he had such gorgeous, green eyes. It was especially unfair that he was using them to look at her like she was the answer to all his prayers.

"I suppose it wouldn't hurt to meet her."

"I really appreciate that, Rosie. Do you like pizza?"

"Love it."

"How about vegetarian?"

"It's not my favorite, I—" Something in his expression stopped her. "Vegetarian is fine."

"Okay great. We'll meet you at the Pizza Parlor at six."

The smile he gave her did crazy things to her heart. Too bad it also did crazy things to her head. She had a feeling she was going to regret this—but she said yes.

"A JOB LOOKING after his disabled sister?" Portia shook her head in dismay. "I was sure that stuff about needing help was just a ploy to ask you out."

Rosie was glad the day was finally at an end. Ever since she'd returned from her coffee with Brant she'd been having trouble focusing.

"If Brant Willington wanted to ask anyone out, it certainly wasn't me. Maybe if you'd gone with him for coffee, you'd have had better luck."

"The last thing I want is to meet a guy or go out on a date, Rosie."

Portia sounded so gravely serious, Rosie stopped counting the stack of fives in her hand.

"Okay. Noted."

"Thank you. Now to get back to the matter of you and Brant—"

"There is no me and Brant. That's what I'm trying to tell you."

"Maybe not yet, but if you're going to be spending time with his sister, then you'll probably be running into him more often as well. Things could happen."

"Not with my luck they won't."

"Have you given yourself a chance? Gone out somewhere you might meet someone?"

"No," she admitted.

"When was the last time you did your hair, got dressed up and went out to the bar with some girlfriends?"

"Um… last year's rodeo, I think."

Portia rolled her eyes. "Tell you what. Give me fifteen minutes with my straightening iron and my makeup bag, before you go for that pizza. You might be surprised what could happen next."

Rosie couldn't deny the idea of a mini-makeover was appealing. "You sure you only need fifteen minutes? It's already five-thirty and I'm supposed to meet him and his sister at the Pizza Parlor at six."

"Well, let's get busy then. I have all my stuff in my purse."

"Your flat iron is in your purse?"

"Isn't everyone's?"

Rosie laughed and Portia joined in.

"It's funny," Portia said. "We've only known each other a couple of days, yet it feels like we've been friends forever."

Rosie's couldn't find her voice to reply. She hadn't realized how much she'd missed having someone the same age to talk to. There was Dakota, of course, but they worked different shifts. Plus, since a particularly painful breakup, Dakota spent almost all her free time at the Whiskers and Paw Pals Animal Rescue.

After Rosie had walked the deposit over to the First Bank of Marietta, Portia herded her into the small restroom at the back of the chocolate shop.

While the flat iron was heating, Portia performed her makeup magic. First she applied foundation and bronzer, and then attacked Rosie's eyes with a series of pencils and brushes and a palette of four shades from pearl to smoky gray.

Even after she'd lined Rosie's lips with colored pencil and filled them in with a luscious berry-scented gloss, she wouldn't let Rosie look in the mirror.

"You have amazing lips Rosie. So plump and such a pretty shape."

"I always thought they looked too puffy."

"Are you kidding? Men love that."

When she tried to sneak a look at the mirror, Portia blocked her. "Wait until I'm done. The hair is the most important part."

Rosie tried to sit patiently. "I wish I'd had time to research Autistic Syndrome before meeting Sara Maria."

"Too bad my sister Wren isn't here. She'd no doubt be able to share all the scientific facts with you. She's like a walking Wikipedia."

Portia removed the elastic band from Rosie's hair and started brushing it out. Now Rosie had to try to be patient *and* not to wince.

"I can't match Wren's knowledge," Portia continued. "But I did read a book by Jodi Picoult once that had a main character with Asperger's Syndrome. As I recall, he would only eat foods of a certain color on certain days, he hated loud noises, and he was married to his daily routines. Any deviation from normal could send him into a total breakdown."

"God, I'm not sure I could handle someone having a total breakdown."

Portia reached for the flat iron. "Me either. I guess you better figure out what she likes and make sure she gets it."

"That doesn't sound like a lot of fun, either." Rosie was beginning to feel really nervous about her upcoming meeting. Why had Brant sounded so sure of her ability to handle his sister? She had no medical training. She'd never even met anyone who was autistic.

Rosie's stomach was a cyclone of anxiety by the time Portia finished with her hair.

"I wish I could lend you some clothes, but even if I had my entire closet with me, your legs are too long and your top is too slender."

"Oh, just call me flat-chested. I can handle it."

Portia groaned. "Tall and slender is a good thing. It means you can wear almost anything. Trust me, I only look good because I know what fashion mistakes to avoid. Hang on. I think I have a scarf in my purse, too. Keep your eyes closed."

Rosie complied. Truth was, she was afraid to look. What if Portia had layered on the makeup to such a degree Rosie would feel embarrassed to go out? Portia was being so helpful and generous. Rosie didn't want to insult her if she didn't like the result.

At the same time, she was not going to meet Brant and his sister looking like one of the Kardashians.

"Okay, here it is." Portia was back, with a scrap of a scarf that felt soft as a cloud around Rosie's neck.

She sat patiently while Portia adjusted the silk until it fell just so. And then she was done.

"Okay. You can open your eyes."

Rosie did. And then she stared.

Was that really her?

Her wild hair had been tamed into soft waves. Whatever Portia had done to her eyes, had made them look double their normal size. And her skin practically glowed.

As for the scarf, it was the perfect added touch that Rosie would never have thought to bother with.

"You are a magician. Or a witch. How did you do this?"

Rosie touched her hair, almost surprised to find that, yes, it was actually attached to her head.

"You crazy girl. It was so easy. And it took just under fourteen minutes I might add, which means you could do this every day if you wanted to."

Rosie forced her gaze away from her reflection. "I wish I could do something to repay you."

The light dimmed in Portia's eyes. For a moment it seemed like she might cry again, but then she busied herself putting away her makeup.

"You already have, Rosie. Trust me."

Chapter Five

B RANT GOT HIS sister to the restaurant a few minutes early, wanting to get her settled before Rosie arrived. This meeting had to go well. Hopefully his sister would take to Rosie as quickly as he had. Once Sara Maria decided she didn't like someone, it was hard to get her to change her mind. The few times he'd brought a woman home to meet his family had been disasters. Sara Maria didn't like the idea of him having a girlfriend, which was why he'd gone to great pains to explain to her that Rosie was going to be *her* friend, not his.

"But how can she be my friend if I've never met her?"

His sister could be too damn logical sometimes. "That's why we're having dinner together. So you can meet her and decide if you'd like to do stuff together. Hiking and shopping maybe."

"What if I don't like her?"

"Then we'll look for someone different. Someone you *do* like."

Sara Maria took a moment to consider that. "Is finding a

friend always this much work?"

He chuckled. Yup, sometimes she drove him crazy and other times she made him laugh.

"Why are you laughing at me?"

"I'm laughing at life. Because you're right. Finding a friend can be a lot of work sometimes. But it's totally worth it. If you find the right person then you can end up being so much happier."

And just as the last word came out of his mouth he saw her.

Or did he?

She looked so very different, he wasn't sure at first.

Her hair was suddenly sleek and tame. And why had he never noticed before that she had such knock-out pouty, pink lips?

Awkwardly he got to his feet and pulled out a chair for her.

"Sara Maria, this is the friend I was telling you about. Her name is Rosie Linn."

"Do you really work at the chocolate shop?" Sara Maria asked the question shyly, ducking her head so Rosie could only see half of her face.

"I really do. I hear your favorite is salted dark chocolate caramels."

"I love them. Brant buys me some every week."

"I know. He's a nice brother, huh?"

When Rosie turned to smile at him, he realized he'd

been staring.

"Is something wrong?" she asked.

"You look—different." He tried to pinpoint why. "No ponytail."

"I have to tie my hair back at work because I handle food."

"Right." He wished she would tie her hair back here, as well. He was being distracted, and that wasn't good. If Sara Maria sensed he was attracted to Rosie his entire plan could backfire.

The server came up to their table then, and thankfully Rosie didn't object when he ordered an extra-large vegetarian pizza for them to share.

While they waited for their food, Rosie took the opportunity to chat with his sister.

"I have a brother, too. His name is Daniel and he's twelve years older than me. He and his wife Glenda live in L.A."

"Brant is ten years older than me. I'm eighteen. Our mother is in heaven. Isn't that right Brant?"

He did his best not to roll his eyes. "Yup."

"And she's not coming back. Not ever. It's like when our dog Prince died. He didn't come back either."

"That's very sad, Sara Maria. I bet you miss your mother. I sure miss mine. My mom and my dad are gone, too."

"We have that in common. It's good for friends to have things in common."

Rosie covered her mouth with her hand, but the crinkles at the corners of her eyes betrayed her smile.

The server brought their pizza and the conversation shifted to food. Sara Maria told Rosie about the documentary she'd watched about meat processing plants. When she started getting into the gorier details, Brant shifted the conversation to movies, which was a much safer topic.

"My favorite last year was *Brooklyn*," Rosie said. "How about you?"

"I really liked that one, too. Brant fell asleep right in the middle."

"To be fair, I was up at five that morning and worked a solid nine hours before driving to Marietta," he defended himself.

"But he liked it in the end. He even cried."

"Tears of exhaustion. Seemed like the damn movie would never end." He winked at Rosie and she smiled, but his literal sister would not let his comment lie.

"You never cried before when you were tired."

"You got me there, sis. Now, anyone want some ice cream for dessert?"

The rest of the evening passed without any major embarrassment and it must have gone all right because when it came time for Rosie to leave she asked if Sara Maria would like to join her on a hike to a waterfall on Copper Mountain the next day.

"Yes," Sara Maria replied, simply.

"Maybe I should come, as well." His conscience wouldn't let him saddle Rosie with his sister until he was sure she could handle her.

"Rosie is supposed to be *my* friend." Sara Maria pursed her lips then added. "But I suppose it's okay if you tag along."

THE SOUND OF an in-coming text message woke Rosie the next morning. Her head felt foggy, thanks to a restless night spent regretting her invitation to take Sara Maria hiking. She'd felt sorry for the young woman, who'd lost her mother so recently and seemed so lost, and the words had just slipped out without her thinking about the wisdom of it all.

She rolled over and grabbed her phone from the nightstand. If she was lucky, Brant was suffering second thoughts too and was contacting her to cancel their plans.

But the message was from Portia.

"Sage told Mom I dropped out. Now Mom is driving to Marietta to talk sense into me. help! What do I say?"

Rosie sat up. She could feel Portia's panicked desperation. *"Tell her you were flunking out anyway?"*

"But she saw my grades. They were pretty good. (shocking, i know.)"

Rosie smiled. Portia liked playing the underachiever. But if she really was a decent student, why not finish her degree? Rosie didn't type what she was thinking, though. Right now Portia needed her support, not her opinion.

"Tell her you're burned out and need a break but plan to return next fall."

"Brilliant! Thx Rosie."

Rosie congratulated herself. She wasn't even out of bed and she'd already solved one problem. Too bad it wasn't one of hers.

Fighting the urge to drop back to sleep, Rosie got up and dressed in jeans and a casual sweatshirt. Neither item was sexy or stylish, but they were practical for a hike. She pushed aside her curtains, revealing blue skies and a clear view to the Gallatin Mountains in the west. A perfect autumn day.

Her heart beat faster.

She was going to see him again today.

With his sister. As a paid companion, no less. This was the farthest thing possible from a date. Not only that, it was the very opposite of the fresh start she had promised herself.

Why, oh why, had she agreed to this again?

She was pretty sure a guy with hunky, broad shoulders and killer, green eyes was to blame.

In the bathroom mirror, she inspected her hair. It still looked nice. *Thank-you, Portia, for using hair spray.* She wouldn't be able to recreate Portia's magic with her makeup, though, which was just as well, since that would have made it look like she was trying too hard.

Huck met her in the kitchen. He nudged his bowl with his nose, then looked at her forlornly.

Rosie scooped out his breakfast and freshened his water.

Although her father had been gone since March, Huck still seemed so sad. He'd always slept in her parents' room and he still did, even though she'd tried placing his favorite blanket at the foot of her bed.

Maybe Huck sensed she was going to leave him soon, too.

Feeling guilty, she stooped to give the dog a hug and a scratch.

Hopefully the new owners, when she found them, would be dog lovers. If not she would find Huck another good home.

As Rosie was putting on a pot of coffee, her phone chimed again.

"How was your night with Cowboy?"

Rosie groaned. The evening had hardly been the X-rated event Portia made it sound like.

She started the coffeemaker then typed out her reply. *"I think I managed to get myself hired as PT babysitter for his sister. I'm taking her for a hike today."*

"Oh. Wow. Good luck to you too then."

Rosie set the phone down trying not to feel disheartened. If Portia had met Brant for pizza last night, no doubt she would have ended up with a date instead of a paid companion job.

Rosie had oatmeal with blueberries for breakfast. When she was finished, she took her second cup of coffee to the front porch, her favorite place to sit and relax, despite the sagging floor boards that threatened to crater any day now.

She snuggled into the cushioned, wicker love seat. In the planter boxes on both sides of the porch, gold and orange chrysanthemums still bloomed brightly, not yet touched by early winter frost.

Rosie put up her feet and took another sip of coffee. She wished she could relax and enjoy the mountain view while she still had one, but with each minute she grew more anxious.

This had been such a bad idea.

She was supposed to be living her life. Not babysitting some hunky cowboy's sister so he could live his.

Fortunately she wasn't committed yet. All she had to do was take Sara Maria on this hike as promised, then tell her brother it wasn't going to work after all. Brant had set this up as a trial run, which proved he had his doubts about the arrangement, as well. He would probably be grateful to her for giving him an out.

Five minutes before their agreed-upon meeting time, she heard the rumble of an approaching vehicle. A gray truck slowed and pulled up across from her house. Brant was in the driver's seat with his sister next to him.

Showtime.

She set down her coffee, then slipped a lead onto Huck's collar. She hadn't thought to ask if Sara Maria like animals. She supposed she was about to find out.

Brant stepped out of the truck first. He had no hat today, and had traded his riding boots for hiking ones, but he still managed to look one-hundred-percent cowboy in his faded jeans and form-fitting western-styled shirt. He squared his broad shoulders to her and nodded.

Rosie's heart thudded and her face pulsed with heat.

Did he have to look so darn... *good?*

He gave her a tentative smile. Was he feeling the same doubts as her about this situation?

Rosie approached cautiously, keeping Huck on a short lead. "This is Huck, he's totally friendly. Is your sister okay with dogs?"

"She loves them. Too much, in fact."

Sara Maria scrambled in front of her brother, beaming. She had a lovely smile. Rosie hadn't caught many glimpses of it the other night.

"Hey there, Huck." Sara Maria spoke gently as she approached the old golden lab.

"Just give him a scratch on his neck. He loves that."

While Sara Maria got acquainted with Huck, Brant glanced around at the house. "Nice place."

"Thanks."

"I saw the *For Sale* sign on the gate. How long has it been on the market?"

"Over six months. My realtor warned me it probably wouldn't sell until I fixed it up a little."

"Some paint would go a long way."

"Yes, but first I need to repair the porch stairs and some of the window casements. It's sort of like a ball of wool, once you start pulling, it just keeps unraveling."

"You should hire someone."

"I've tried but our handyman has been really busy this summer... or so he says. I have a suspicion he doesn't want me to sell. He and Dad were best friends—I think he's even more attached to this house than I am."

While they'd been talking, Sara Maria had found one of Huck's tennis balls and was playing fetch with him. As the conversation lapsed into a natural pause she asked, "Can Huck come with us on our hike?"

"Try to stop him. I thought we'd walk along Trespass Creek to a pretty spectacular waterfall. It's one of my favorite hikes, about three miles in total. Sound okay?"

Brant looked at his sister assessingly. "Sounds like something Sara Maria can handle. We'll need water. A can of bear spray to be safe."

"I've got both, plus some trail mix in my backpack and a basic first aid kit." She slipped the light pack over her shoulders, refusing Brant's outstretched hand. "I'm good."

Sara Maria turned out to be an enthusiastic hiker. Once they left the yard and joined the trail, just beyond Miracle Lake, Sara Maria took the lead and Huck was right up with her, displaying more energy than Rosie had seen from him in months.

Brant hung back with Rosie and soon they'd left the meadow behind and were climbing through trees with the slow-moving creek to their left.

The well-worn path was spongy underfoot, strewn with old pine needles and yellow cottonwood leaves. Rosie savored each breath of the autumn-scented air. She loved this season, even though she dreaded the upcoming winter.

It wasn't so much the cold and the snow she didn't like, as the feeling of being cut off from the rest of the world, a feeling that had been exacerbated when living with her shut-in father.

"Seems like my sister and your dog have bonded."

"Maybe you should hire Huck instead of me."

"Cute."

"I'm not kidding. He's nonunionized and his rates are super affordable."

Brant's eyes glinted with humor. "I'd take you up on that, but pets aren't allowed at the care home."

Since his sister was far enough ahead that she couldn't hear their conversation, Rosie asked, "Does she really need to live there? She seems fine to me. A little socially awkward, perhaps, but perfectly capable otherwise."

"That's because everything is happening according to plan. As long as we follow a routine and nothing unexpected happens, you're right, Sara Maria almost seems normal."

"And when it doesn't—how does she react?"

He grimaced. "Total breakdown."

Brant's answer was characteristically brief.

But Rosie needed to know more. "What is one of Sara Maria's breakdowns like?"

Brant considered for a moment. "She collapses. No matter where we are—in the house, on the street, in a church—she just falls to the floor, the street, the ground, whatever. Then she covers her ears and starts making this awful, high-pitched sound."

"But she isn't violent?"

"No."

That was a relief. "Has she ever hurt herself in one of her episodes?"

"Not really... though she came close to getting run over once when she had a fit in a crosswalk."

"That sounds scary."

"Fortunately she was with Mom. Mom had a way of talking to Sara Maria—she could always get her to calm down fairly quickly." Brant's eyes clouded. "While everything I say or do riles her up more."

"Has Sara Maria had any breakdowns recently?"

"Last major one was when we found out about Mom's car accident. We were out for pizza when a state trooper called me. My sister freaked out so badly I had to phone 911. She was hospitalized for a few weeks while I worked out arrangements for her to move to the care home in Marietta."

"How awful. For both of you."

He swallowed. "I miss Mom lots. But it's harder for Sara Maria. You heard her talk about Mom being in heaven? Well, she says stuff like that every single time I see her." He pulled at the collar of his shirt, as if it was choking him. "I know she's grieving. But, God, I wish she'd give it a rest already."

"She really pushes your buttons. Do you think it's on purpose?"

"Nah. She can't help it. I know that. I try to be patient. But, hell, I'd rather deal with the most stubborn horse in the world than try to figure out my sister."

Chapter Six

ROSIE HELD OUT her arms for balance as she crossed the wobbly log bridge over Trespass Creek. During spring runoff, the crossing could be perilous but this time of year the water level was low and the current lazy. Still, Rosie was impressed with how confidently Sara Maria moved, taking long, confident strides with no fear.

The water was shallow enough for Huck to splash right in. He took a long drink, then bounded to the other side, running to catch up with Sara Maria.

"Your sister is in really good shape." Rosie was trying not to huff and puff too much.

She hiked these trails often. But not at this pace. It was a little embarrassing to be having trouble keeping pace with Brant's sister.

"Better than I thought," Brant admitted. "She's just powering up this trail."

Rosie noticed Brant was having no trouble either. "So what sort of work do you do at Three Bars Ranch?"

"A bit of everything."

As they drew nearer to the waterfall, the sound of rushing water was growing louder. Keeping an eye on Sara Maria to make sure she didn't get too far ahead, Rosie asked, "Such as?"

"My favorite is working with the young horses. This week I'm training a three-year-old filly—smartest horse I've ever met. Her name is Sweet Pea Runner and she's got amazing talent. If I had more time—"

His words died away as they rounded a curve in the trail to a sweeping view of a twenty-foot waterfall. Ahead of them Sara Maria had come to a dead stop.

Rosie went to stand beside her, a little nervous in case this was the sort of thing that might "set her off."

"What do you think?"

Eyes fixed on the waterfall, Sara Maria said reverently, "This is one of the most beautiful things I've ever seen."

"It's incredible." Brant passed them, walking to the edge of the embankment and gazing up at the water, which cascaded through a picturesque series of giant stone steps into a large pool at their feet, beyond which the creek continued at a more sedate pace down the mountain.

Right now the sun shone through an opening in the tall, rough-barked, pine trees, illuminating a large flat rock at the side of the crystal-clear water.

Before her parents became ill, this had been their favorite place to take Rosie for a hike and a picnic. With the twelve-year age gap between her and Daniel, Rosie had grown up like an only child, which probably explained why she'd felt so compelled to look after first her mom, then her dad, in their final years.

"My mom called this picnic rock," Rosie said. "Since it catches the noon sun, it's a nice, warm spot to sit and have lunch." Even as she said this, she was shrugging off her back pack and sinking down for a rest. After the exertion of hiking, it was a pleasure to feel the heat from the rock seep up through her body.

Sara Maria joined her, sitting close to the edge, where a soft mist rose up from the waterfall. A slow smile spread over her face.

"This feels good."

"Better than a facial," Rosie agreed. She pulled the food from her pack. "I didn't bring much, just some cheese and crackers and trail mix. It's a special blend Sage makes at the chocolate shop with flakes of coconut, hazelnuts, and chocolate covered dried cherries."

"I would like some of that," Sara Maria said.

Rosie handed her one of the three plastic bags she'd packed as well as a bottle of water. "Brant?"

He was staring at her and the look in his eyes made her swallow, hard.

"Your hair." He reached down to touch a strand. "It looks pretty with the sunlight dancing on it."

She swallowed a second time, captivated by the look of admiration in his eyes. But then his gaze drifted toward his sister and he frowned.

"I'm going to explore the area a bit," Brant said, his tone clipped. "I'll be back soon."

She watched him disappear along the path that led to the top of Copper Mountain. What would have happened just then if they'd been alone?

No. She couldn't let herself think that way about him.

Briefly she closed her eyes, savoring the warmth of the midday sun on her skin. Only her need to keep an eye on Sara Maria prevented her from giving in to the urge to take a nap. Brant's sister seemed perfectly calm and content, though, as she munched on the trail mix.

When she was finished eating, Sara Maria spread out flat on the warm stone. "I wish I could stay here forever."

"It is lovely. But in another hour the sun will have moved behind the trees and you'd start to feel cold."

"Anyway Brant would never let me stay. I have to go back to that place."

Rosie glanced around, slightly uneasy that she still couldn't see any sign of Brant. "You don't like the care home?"

"Doesn't matter. I don't have a choice. I'm not allowed to live on the ranch with my brother. Besides, he wouldn't like that. He thinks I'm weird."

"I haven't known him very long, but Brant seems pretty nice, as brothers go."

"That's because he promised Mom he'd take care of me."

It was an astute observation, fitting what Rosie herself had concluded. Whatever her challenges, Sara Maria certainly seemed quite bright and observant.

"You must miss your mom."

"People say she's in heaven, like that's a good thing. I don't want her in heaven. I want her here."

Rosie was floundering for a reply when, with impeccable timing, Huck emerged from the woods and joined Sara Maria on the sunbaked rock. She put her arm around the dog, not seeming to mind that he was damp from his romp in the creek.

Rosie felt a thick sadness rise up from her heart and lodge in her throat. She knew what grief was, how it could shroud all that was good and bright in the world.

"It will get easier." The platitude was actually true, but Rosie could tell Sara Maria didn't believe it any more than Rosie had when well-meaning friends had said it to her.

"WHAT DO YOU think?" Brant admired Rosie's glowing skin as they paused to chat on her front porch. Sara Maria was waiting for them in the truck, her head resting against the closed window. The exercise and fresh air had been good for her.

As far as he was concerned the day couldn't have gone better.

He watched as Rosie released Huck from his lead. A

strand of her curly hair fell in her eyes as she did this, and she pushed it aside impatiently when she straightened.

"Will you take the job?"

Rosie hesitated.

And he agonized.

He liked Rosie. She was easy to be around and she made him laugh. More importantly, he could tell his sister liked her.

The arrangement was practically perfect, except for one thing.

"You don't want to do it, do you?"

"Not really."

He'd expected that answer, but hearing her deliver it made him realize how much he'd hoped she'd say yes. "You can't handle my sister?"

She glanced at the truck, then back to him. "I like your sister. I'd be happy to spend time with her. But as I said, I'm moving soon."

He surveyed the property that had been on the market for over six months. It was easy to see why it hadn't sold, given all the work that was needed.

An idea sparked, one that might help both of them.

"What would you say to a deal? I help you fix up your house in exchange for you getting my sister out of that home a few times a week."

She glanced from him to the house, her expression contemplative.

"Hm…do you have handyman experience?"

He laughed. "My job at the ranch requires me to do a little of everything, including painting and construction."

"What about plumbing? I've got leaking taps and a temperamental toilet inside."

When it came to temperamental, he'd take a toilet over his sister any day. "Not a problem."

"Well… I work at the chocolate shop on Friday, Saturday and Monday. So I probably won't have time to take Sara Maria out on those days."

"How about we keep things fluid? You let me know whenever you have a block of free time to spend with my sister. And I'll work on your house whenever I can get away from the ranch."

"That sounds reasonable. Are there other things your sister likes to do besides hike?"

"Movies. But we do that on Friday night." He struggled to think of more suggestions. "Maybe you could take her shopping?"

"Sure. Sara Maria will probably have her own ideas, too. I'll ask her next time we get together."

He grinned. "You don't know what a load you've taken off me. Thanks, Rosie. I'll let the people at the care home know about our arrangement so you won't have any problems when you go to pick her up."

He was so happy he felt like hugging her. But he doubted she'd find that appropriate. "Can I get your cell phone number?"

She dug her phone out of her pocket and, as they exchanged contact information, he found himself wondering if she would have given him her number under different circumstances.

WHILE CLEANING UP after her solitary Sunday dinner, Rosie realized she hadn't seen Huck for a few hours. She checked his food bowl. His evening rations were untouched.

When he didn't come at her summons she went to her parents' bedroom.

Generally she avoided this room, except for the occasional quick dust and vacuum. She always felt sad when she saw the familiar old coverlet on their queen-sized bed, so smooth now that her father wasn't here to crumple it.

The night tables on either side of the bed looked foreign as well, absent their former piles of novels, magazines and crossword puzzles. Worst of all was the too-tidy desk in the corner where her father had written all his thrillers.

Rosie had been forced to purge all traces of her parents' occupation when she'd put the house on the market. Even so, Huck still liked this room best. And, sure enough, she found the old dog curled up on the thick rug on her father's side of the bed.

The lab raised his head when she called his name, but didn't stand.

"What's wrong boy? Are you tired from our hike?" She sure was. "Come on, I'll give you some gravy tonight as a special treat."

Gravy was Huck's favorite. And though his ears perked at the word, he still didn't stir.

"Okay. Be stubborn. But if you haven't eaten your food by the morning, I'm going to take you to see Dr. Sullivan."

She could have sworn Huck cringed when she named the vet, but he refused to be moved. So she gave him a good scratch then went back to the family room. She pulled out the pages she'd been working on earlier. Her brother had sent her an outline for the next scene in their TV pilot. As usual he needed her help to jazz up the dialogue.

She was deep into the story when her cell phone rang.

Her first thought—okay, hope—was that it might be Brant. But it was Portia and she sounded stressed.

"Rosie! Thank God you're at home. Can I come over?"

"Sure."

Rosie recited her address then warned. "It's about a mile from your aunt's house."

"No worries. Dawson's out on patrol tonight. He said he could come back and give me a lift."

Sage's husband had given up a successful rodeo career to become a deputy about five years ago. Rosie would never forget the way Dawson had courted Sage, trying to convince her he was a changed man from the one she'd met when they were both on the rodeo circuit.

Sage had taken a lot of persuading, but she'd finally agreed. Rosie was pretty sure it was a gamble she had never regretted.

"That sounds perfect, Portia. I'll put on the porch light. You'll see a *For Sale* sign on the front gate, too."

"Thanks. Oh, and one more favor? Could I—stay overnight?"

Despite her surprise, Rosie was quick to agree. She hadn't had a friend for a sleepover since she was a teenager. But Portia sounded pretty anxious. Perhaps the visit from her mom hadn't gone well.

Thirty minutes later, when Portia arrived, her eyes were red and her skin was blotchy, confirming Rosie's guess that there'd been some family drama.

Rosie gave her a hug. "Are you okay? I think I better open a bottle of wine."

"You wouldn't believe what the past twenty-four hours have been like."

Rosie carried a bottle of red and two glasses to the family room. She was relieved when Huck made the effort to come inspect their visitor. It was good to see him moving, at least. After a few exchanges of sniffs on his part, and pats on Portia's, he went to the kitchen and chowed down his dinner.

"So where's your mom?" Rosie asked, as she opened the bottle and poured two glasses.

"At Aunt Sage's." Portia settled cross-legged into the far

corner of the sofa, then grabbed one of the plump pillows and clutched it to her middle like a life preserver. "We just had the biggest fight. I had to get out of there."

Rosie settled at the other end of the sofa and took a sip of the wine. "I guess she's really angry you dropped out of college?"

"Yes. Very. She keeps asking me *why, why, why?*" Portia ran a finger round the lip of her wine glass. "She won't believe me when I say I'm burned out. Even when I promised to go back next year, she would not let it go."

"Maybe she senses there's more to the story. Mothers have instincts about these things."

Portia looked at her, pained.

"Don't worry. I'm not going to nag you, too. Obviously you aren't ready to talk about whatever happened."

"Thank you." Some of the tension left Portia's shoulders. She brought the wine glass to her lips, then set it down. "Mom and I don't have fights very often. I really hate this."

"She'll get over her anger," Rosie predicted.

"Maybe. But I don't think she'll ever stop being disappointed." Portia sank back into the sofa and glanced around the room. "This is cozy. I like it."

"During the day we have a great view of the mountains." Rosie gestured to the floor to ceiling windows on the west-facing wall.

"Do you mind living on your own?"

"I don't love it," she admitted.

If it wasn't for Huck, she probably wouldn't have lasted a week after her father died.

"I should warn you—I have an ulterior motive in asking. Since it looks like I'm going to be staying in Marietta for a while I need a place to stay. Aunt Sage's house isn't that big. Not to mention her kids get up really early and they're pretty noisy. Is there any chance you'd like a roommate?"

Rosie had never considered the idea before. But she immediately liked it. "That could be fun. Want to see the spare bedroom?"

Portia did and immediately announced it was perfect.

It wasn't. It was small and the walls were painted an odd blue that had looked like a soft grey in the can.

"Are you sure this will be okay? My parents' room is much bigger."

"Oh, I wouldn't feel right about that."

Rosie was relieved. Though the master bedroom was clean and ready to be occupied, it would have felt strange to have Portia sleeping in it.

"I'm serious when I say this is perfect." Portia sank onto the bed and the springs let out a loud, rusty squeak.

They both laughed and Rosie almost joked that she'd know if Portia brought a boyfriend home. But Portia had already made it clear she wasn't interested in dating. And she'd sounded serious.

Once they'd agreed on a rent Portia insisted on writing her first check immediately.

"I love Aunt Sage, Dawson, and the kids. But it will be a relief to get away from family. To have some space to think without anyone hovering."

Rosie wondered what it was Portia needed to think about. She smoothed her hand over the quilted coverlet. "You'll have lots of peace and quiet here. Maybe too much."

"I doubt if that's possible." Portia lifted her chin and pointedly changed the subject. "Say, you went hiking today, didn't you? Did your hot cowboy come along?"

Rosie rolled her eyes. "Yes. But his hotness was irrelevant. It wasn't a date. He wanted me to spend time his sister. See if I could handle her, I guess."

"Obviously I need to ply you with wine if I want the juicy bits." Portia refilled Rosie's wine glass. "So. Details, please."

"The hike was fine. His sister really connected to Huck. I think she liked me okay as well."

"So you came second to the dog? Nice."

Rosie laughed. "Sara Maria is pretty cool, actually. Different, but cool."

"And the cowboy?"

Words were inadequate to describe what Rosie thought of Brant. He'd caught her eye from the beginning, but the more she saw of him, the more she liked him.

"Brant's a good guy. But pretty clueless where his sister is concerned."

Portia let out an exasperated sigh. "I'm sure his sister is a very nice person. But can we forget about her for a moment? I want to know how you feel about the cowboy. Is there dating potential?"

Yes. And then some. But being around Brant was like staring in the window of a fine Parisian Patisserie when she had not so much as a euro in her purse.

In other words, torture, of the most exquisite kind.

"You don't need to answer," Portia said. "Your expression says it all. Want a glass of ice water to cool off?"

"I'll stick with the wine, thank you. It doesn't matter how I feel, though. He'll never ask me out—" She put up a hand to stop Portia from interrupting. "And if he did, what's the point? I'll be living in L.A. soon."

"Not all relationships have to be permanent, Rosie. You could try dating him for the simple reason that it would be fun."

"Fun. Hm. Interesting concept."

Portia clapped her hands. "I know what we should do. We need to go online and buy you a few new outfits. So you'll have something to wear when he asks you out."

Rosie didn't bother arguing. No doubt if Portia decided she was going to date a guy, she made it happen. Life didn't work that way for Rosie.

But new clothes were a good idea. She'd need them when she moved.

Chapter Seven

DESPITE HAVING EXCHANGED contact information with him the previous day, Rosie was surprised to receive a text message from Brant the next morning.

"Can I phone you?"

The longer Rosie stared at the text message, the faster her heart raced. They'd settled their business last night, so why would he contact her now? Could Portia be right? Was Brant actually going to ask her out?

She thought about the new skirt, jeans, and cute tops she'd ordered last night. Thank God, Portia had insisted on express delivery.

"Sure."

She took her phone to the porch. Portia had just left to walk to her aunt's and pack up the rest of her things, so Rosie was alone with Huck. The golden lab seemed to be in a happier space today. Not only had he eaten all his breakfast, but he'd been keen to go on a morning walk along the Marietta River.

Now he was sleeping in a patch of sunshine on the far corner of the porch.

Rosie settled next to him, resting her back against the porch railing. She ran her fingers along Huck's back. His thick coat felt bristly and slightly oily.

She wondered how long it would take for Brant to call her back.

It seemed like an hour, but was probably only ten minutes, before the phone finally rang and the name "Brant" appeared on the screen.

She took a deep breath and tried to sound casual. "Hey there."

"Hey."

There was an awkward pause, during which time Rosie mentally composed her response for when he asked her out. She didn't want to sound overly eager. But not disinterested, either.

"Um, I'm calling to ask a favor. Are you at work?"

Rosie frowned. This wasn't the opening she'd expected from him. "I normally would be, but I traded shifts with Dakota this week."

"I had a call from the care home this morning." There was a long hesitation, then he added, "Sara Maria had an episode at breakfast."

"Oh, no. What set her off? Is she okay?"

"I didn't get the details. I gather she's calmed down now, but the staff want someone—a family member or a friend—to check on her."

And to think she'd hoped he was calling to ask her out.

Rosie felt like groaning. "Let me guess—you want me to go?"

"I've got a hell of a lot of work lined up here, plus I'm almost an hour drive away. I know it's not part of our agreement."

"No, it isn't. Plus, Sara Maria has only known me a few days. That hardly qualifies me as her friend."

"Maybe not to the average person. But Sara Maria really likes you, Rosie. She flat out told me. And she doesn't like many people."

Rosie couldn't help but feel moved by that. Remembering the intense sadness she'd sensed in the other woman, her conscience wouldn't let her say no now, even though her head told her she'd be smart to stick to the rules they'd set out the previous night.

"I'm not that busy." A lie, since Daniel wanted her script changes before noon. "I suppose I could go check on her."

"I'll make it up to you. I've asked my boss for some time off so I can work on your house. I promise when I'm finished with the repairs and painting, buyers will be lined up to make an offer."

It always came down to commercial transactions with Brant. She wondered if he'd even registered the fact that she was a woman, around his age, and possibly someone he might date.

"I don't have a clue what I'm going to say to your sister."

"You'll do better than I would."

Rosie didn't doubt that.

THE CARE HOME was only four blocks away and Rosie was halfway there when she remembered how Sara Maria had connected with Huck. Deciding she needed all the help she could get, she retraced her steps home and leashed up her dog.

"I know you've already had one walk today, but you won't mind another, will you, boy? Sara Maria needs you."

Huck cocked his head, conveying his confusion, but he followed her good-naturedly.

Sara Maria was sitting on a bench by the main door to the care home when they arrived. One of the nurses was seated beside her, talking in a soothing tone.

Sara Maria's expression was impassive, but the moment she spied Huck, she came alive, smiling and bounding up from the bench.

"Huck! That's a good boy. Did you come to see me?" Totally ignoring Rosie, Sara Maria bent down and hugged the old dog.

This left Rosie free to approach the nurse. Up close, she could read the name pinned to her blouse. "Hi, Nadia, I'm Rosie Linn."

"Nice to meet you." The nurse offered her hand. "Sara Maria's brother explained that you'd be coming by occasionally to spend time with his sister. I'm glad you could make it today. She had a rough morning."

Rosie glanced over her shoulder. Sara Maria had buried her face in Huck's neck, and the cheerful lab seemed perfectly fine with it.

She turned back to Nadia. "What happened?"

"We had a new aide start today. She didn't read the charts before she served breakfast. As soon as Sara Maria saw the bacon on her plate, she went ballistic."

Rosie shivered. "Did she hurt anyone?"

"No. She just crumpled onto the floor, covered her ears with her hands and started moaning. She stayed like that for almost half an hour. Sara Maria has had some previous episodes during her adjustment phase, but we've never seen her this distraught before."

"Poor thing," Rosie murmured, her gaze trained on the young woman, hugging Huck now like she would never let him go.

"We tried to comfort her but she wouldn't let any of us touch her. Finally she calmed down enough to listen to me and when I suggested we sit outside for a while, she agreed. We'd just settled on the bench when you arrived."

Rosie swallowed nervously at the expectant look Nadia gave her.

"I'm not sure how to handle her either," she admitted. "But as you can see, she really likes my dog."

"So many of our guests love animals. Unfortunately there are others with allergies so it isn't feasible to allow pets in the building."

"We'll stay outside." Rosie assured her. "Maybe go for a short walk if Sara Maria is up for it."

"I am," Sara Maria said.

She was a lot more aware of what was going on around her than she let on.

"Fresh air and exercise will be just the thing," Nadia agreed. "Will you be back for lunch?"

"We will," Rosie said at the same time that Sara Maria gave a vehement shake of her head.

"A *vegetarian* lunch." Nadia elaborated.

"Promise?" Sara Maria asked.

"Definitely. That poor aide has certainly learned her lesson where your diet is concerned."

The slight smile on Sara Maria's face was the only sign Rosie had seen so far that she did actually have a sense of humor. Once Nadia was gone, Rosie suggested a walk along the river path to the rodeo grounds.

"Okay. Can I hold Huck's leash?"

"Of course. I think he likes you better anyway." And it was true. When Sara Maria was around, Huck only had eyes for her. As they strolled, Sara Maria seemed so normal and calm. Rosie couldn't reconcile the woman before her with the sort of behavior Nadia had described.

Rosie decided to broach the subject in a straight forward manner.

"This morning, when the new aide brought you your

breakfast—did you consider simply telling her she'd made a mistake? You could have asked her to take it away and bring you something else."

Sara Maria thought about this for a few moments. "I didn't plan on going all crazy, Rosie. It just... happened. I wish it wouldn't. I hate being weird."

"How do the breakdowns come on? Do you have any warning, or does it just come over you in a rush?"

"It happens fast. First my head and my chest feel tight, and it's hard to breathe. The next second it's like a black cloud is swirling around me and every noise hits my head like a blow from a hammer. It's worse if someone tries to touch me." She shuddered.

"That sounds awful."

"It is."

"What would your mother do when this happened to you? How was she able to help you?"

"It was something about her voice. And she would hold me in a way that felt right."

"So your Mom could talk to you and touch you?"

Sara Maria nodded. Her green eyes—a paler version of her brother's—filled with tears. Rosie longed to hug her. But what felt natural and right to her, wouldn't be perceived that way by Sara Maria.

How was she ever going to help this woman? Was it even possible?

ROSIE HAD JUST emailed her script revisions to her brother, when she heard a vehicle pull up in front of her house. She ran out to the porch. Sage was helping Portia unload two suitcases and several bags of groceries from the back of her SUV. Rosie called out hello, then went to peek in on baby Braden, fast asleep in his car seat. Gosh, he was the cutest thing.

"So nice of you to let Portia move in for a while," Sage said.

Her red hair was in a messy updo and she was wearing skinny jeans and a grey t-shirt. Even in such simple attire, she glowed with health and a natural beauty Rosie envied.

"It'll be nice for me to have some company."

Sage laughed. "I think Portia was getting too much company at my place. I love my kids, but they do make the place chaotic. And speaking of kids, I need to pick up Savannah from school now."

"Thanks for everything, Aunt Sage." Portia gave her a hug before she drove off. Then she turned to her new roommate. "Here I am. And I brought food. I hope you like taco salad?"

"Love it." Rosie helped her cart in her belongings and the bags of groceries. "Sage seems okay with you moving out of her place."

"She said all the polite stuff about me being welcome to stay with her as long as I wanted. But honestly, she looked relieved when I told her I'd already given you my first month's rent." Portia popped a carton of almond milk into the fridge. "I guess I wasn't the only one feeling a little crowded."

"Did she decide on your work schedule?"

Portia nodded. "It's somewhat flexible but I'll work most weekday afternoons from two until closing, as well as a few evenings. Sage wants to start hosting after-hour events at her store. Chocolate tastings, truffle-making courses, that sort of thing."

"Really?" Rosie had been trying to talk her boss into doing this for almost a year.

"Aunt Sage told me this was all your idea. I guess with getting married, and then having a baby, she was too overwhelmed to tackle it. But now that I'm here she'd like to give it a try—as long as she doesn't have to do any of the work. What do you say, Rosie—will you help me plan the first event?"

"Seriously? Absolutely yes! How exciting!"

"I'm glad you think so. I feel overwhelmed to be honest. I'm so new to the business. I'm not sure where to start."

"Don't worry. I've got lots of ideas. What do you think about a wine and chocolate pairing event?"

"Ohhh... I love the sound of that!"

"We can partner with our local wine store. Events like this will put Copper Mountain Chocolates on the map. So many tourists drive by Marietta on their way to Yellowstone National Park. I can imagine a day when they stop into

Marietta just to shop at our store."

"Look at you, you're practically vibrating with energy," Portia teased. "Now I see why Aunt Sage is so worried about losing you."

"She is?" Sage had been nothing but supportive of Rosie's plans to move to her brother's and start a new career in L.A.

"Duh. Of course."

"She's never said anything."

"How could she? Sage doesn't want to hold you back."

Rosie wasn't sure how she felt about that. It was nice to know she was valued by her employer. But she didn't like the idea of leaving Sage in the lurch, either. "At least Sage has you, now. In a few months you'll know everything I do."

"I hope I'm a quick learner. But I'll never replace you, Rosie." Portia opened a couple random cabinet doors. "Where do you keep your frying pans? I'd like to fry the seasoned beef for our taco salad."

Rosie pointed to the drawer next to the oven. While Portia prepared the beef, Rosie chopped lettuce, tomatoes, avocados, and crunched some corn chips. Fifteen minutes later, their taco salads were ready. And they were delicious.

"Bonus roommate points to you for being such a good cook."

"It's a Carrigan thing. I learned from my mom, who learned from my Grandma Bramble. My sister Wren isn't a bad cook either, though she'd rather be reading."

"My parents worked long hours, so when I was growing up we ate a lot of takeout. I've never been interested in cooking myself—unless the recipe calls for chocolate."

Portia laughed. "How on earth do you stay so slim?"

Rosie told her about her one sweet a day rule. "But if you keep preparing these awesome meals, I may need to add a serious workout to my regime as well."

She got up from the table, intending to help herself to a bit more salad. That was when she noticed Portia had hardly touched her portion. "What's wrong?"

"Not as hungry as I thought I was. I'll put this in the fridge and eat it later."

Rosie pointed out the drawer with the plastic wrap, then casually mentioned her conversation with Brant that morning, and the favor she'd agreed to do for him.

Portia eyes grew rounder and rounder as Rosie explained about the meltdown.

"Crap. Brant's sister sounds like a real handful. Maybe I shouldn't have encouraged you to take that job."

"I don't mind. I just feel so sorry for her. She seems lost without her mother. Not only is Brant clueless, but I don't think he even wants to try to figure her out."

"Why do you say that?"

"Think about it. He said he was too far away and too busy with his job to spend more time with his sister. But he seems to have lots of time to fix my house in exchange for *me* spending time with Sara Maria."

"Oh. Good point."

Even after their conversation had moved on to planning the chocolate and wine tasting event, Rosie found her thoughts occasionally straying back to Brant. Her insight into his character should have made her like him less, and yet it didn't.

It seemed to Rosie this was a very dangerous sign.

Chapter Eight

AFTER LUNCH ON Tuesday, Rosie drove to the May Bell Care Home in Marietta with some trepidation. Not counting their short walk on Monday, this would be her first afternoon alone with Sara Maria, without Brant present as a buffer. What would they do?

The weather wasn't cooperating.

The temperature had plunged last night, and bundles of clouds were pressing down from the mountains to the north. The smell of rain was in the air, though no drops had yet fallen.

At the care home, the staff was very friendly and happy to see her. A young aide named Brenna told her to wait in the main sitting area, and only a few minutes later Sara Maria appeared wearing jeans and a sweatshirt and carrying her rain jacket.

Even with no makeup and her fine blonde hair pulled back in a ponytail, she looked very pretty. Her expression was serious, tinged with caution. At Rosie's friendly greeting however, she relaxed slightly.

"What would you like to do today? The weather looks a little iffy, but we could go for a walk along the river, and then pop into the Java Café for some tea and a muffin. How does that sound?"

Sara Maria shrugged. "Okay."

Rosie studied her face. "Is there something else you'd rather do?"

"Does it have to be outside?"

"No."

"Then... I'd like to bake some pies."

It took a moment for Rosie to process this. "Pies. Like pastry and fruit—that sort of pie?"

Sara Maria nodded.

"Well." This was the last thing she'd expected. And she wasn't sure this was the sort of "stimulation" Brant expected for his sister. But there was no denying the look of expectation in Sara Maria's eyes. "I have to warn you—I'm no cook. And I'm definitely not a baker."

"That's okay. I know how to make a pie. I don't need any help."

Maybe she did. Maybe she didn't. But Rosie supposed it didn't matter, as long as Sara Maria was happy. "I suppose we can use my kitchen. Sound okay to you?"

Sara Maria smiled.

And that was enough to convince Rosie she'd made the right decision. "What do you need to make a pie?"

"Flour, a bit of vinegar, and some vegetable shortening,"

Sara Maria said. "Plus fruit for the filling."

"I have several bags of rhubarb and raspberries in my freezer." Her next door neighbor had a huge garden and was always bringing Rosie produce she had no idea what to do with. "Would that work?"

"Yes. Do you have the other things?"

"Not the vegetable shortening. But are you sure you want to make the crust from scratch? We could buy one of those frozen crusts."

Sara Maria shook her head vigorously, her expression appalled.

"Okay. No frozen crusts."

They stopped at the market on the way home to pick up the vegetable shortening. At the last moment Rosie added a small bag of pastry flour.

"I can't remember the last time I did any baking. The flour at home might be rancid."

"Buy more flour," Sara Maria said. "I want to make lots of pies."

"Lots of pies as in… two?"

Sara Maria took a moment to consider. "Maybe six."

"Whoa. Are you serious?"

Sara Maria exchanged the one pound bag for the five. Apparently she was.

THE RAIN STARTED fifteen minutes later, just as they were

letting themselves inside through the back entrance. Rosie dropped the sack containing the flour and the shortening on the counter while Sara Maria said hello to Huck, who had made the effort to greet them at the door.

Once she'd finished petting Huck to his satisfaction, Sara Maria washed her hands and asked for a tour of the kitchen. Methodically Rosie opened each of the cabinet doors so Sara Maria could see what was what. When she was done, Sara Maria wrinkled her nose.

"You have things in the wrong places. When we're finished with the pies I can reorder your cabinets."

Rosie didn't know whether to be insulted or to laugh. "We've organized things this way for years and it works fine for me."

"You don't cook. How do you know it works?"

"I may not cook, but I heat food in the microwave. And then I wash my dishes in the dishwasher."

"Yes. And wouldn't it be a good idea if your dishes were closer to the dishwasher? And if you kept your glasses near the fridge?"

"Hm."

"I'll fix it for you. But first I'll make the pies."

"Do you want anything to drink first?"

"No."

"Do you want me to help?"

"No."

A little bemused, Rosie settled on a stool at the end of

the butcher block island and just watched.

What she saw amazed her.

First Sara Maria pulled out every pie plate Rosie's mother had owned—a total of five, not six—as well as a bowl, a knife, the vinegar, and the measuring cups. Then she set out the flour and the shortening.

Sara Maria moved about the kitchen as if she'd known it for years. Not once did she open the wrong cabinet door. Not once did she hesitate over how much of something to add.

In less than thirty minutes she had ten discs of pastry dough wrapped in plastic, which she placed in the fridge to cool.

"We need to let the dough rest for thirty minutes. Maybe I'll play with Huck now."

Huck was only too happy to oblige with this plan. He soon had Sara Maria rolling on the floor with him as they fought over Huck's favorite pull-toy. Then, oblivious to the light drizzle, Sara Maria went out to the fenced-in back yard and threw Huck's tennis ball to the far corner. Huck bounded for it, retrieving it as proudly as a gold ribbon at a track and field event.

But would he give it back to Sara Maria?

Oh, no.

Soon they were tussling on the back deck, with Sara Maria laughing until she was in tears.

Until that moment she had seemed not quite human to

Rosie. Too detached, too clinical, too… cool. But Huck was able to access a part of Sara Maria's humanity that few people—certainly not herself, or Brant—were privy to.

Finally worn out from all the activity, Huck went to his water bowl and began slurping. Sara Maria stretched out on the deck for a moment. Then she sighed and stood up and came inside.

"Time to roll out the dough."

"Can I help?"

"You can heat the oven to 375 degrees if you like."

"You sure you can trust me with that?"

Sara Maria paused to stare at her for a moment. Then slowly she smiled. "I guess I'll find out."

Rosie smiled back, then set the dial as she'd been instructed while Sara Maria washed her hands, yet again.

When Sara Maria asked where the rolling pin was, Rosie had to shrug. She hadn't seen it since her mother died. But it didn't take Sara Maria long to flush it out and as soon as Rosie laid eyes on the scarred wooden utensil she was flooded with childhood memories of her mother baking pies for Thanksgiving and Christmas holidays. She remembered being given small balls of dough to play with… and how grimy they had looked when she was done with them.

Expertly Sara Maria dusted flour onto the counter and the roller, before unwrapping one of the pastry disks and dusting it, too. Her hands moved with elegance and confidence as she gently coaxed the disk into a soft sheet of paper-thin pastry. As soon as she settled it over one of the pie plates, the dough obligingly sank into the proper position.

"That's wonderful, Sara Maria. You make it look so easy." But Rosie knew better.

She could just imagine the way the dough would stick and clump under her hands. She'd end up with flour all over the kitchen, and pies that looked like they'd been made by someone in kindergarten.

Four more times Sara Maria repeated her magic show, transforming lumps of dough into silky-soft pastry.

Then she prepared the filling.

Rosie pulled out her bags of frozen rhubarb and raspberries. "Are you going to make some of each flavor?"

"No. I'll mix them together, along with some corn starch, sugar, and orange zest." Sara Maria snagged one of the oranges from the fruit bowl on the counter, then pulled out another kitchen utensil Rosie hadn't seen in a long time.

Apparently it was an orange zester, because soon tiny slivers of orange peel had accumulated in a pile on the counter and a sweet citrus aroma was teasing Rosie's nose and taste buds.

Sara Maria piled each pie plate high with the fruity mixture, then she repeated her pastry magic and produced covers for each of the pies. For her final trick, she pinched the top crust to the bottom, creating a beautiful, wavy pattern like the kind Rosie had seen in the very best bake shops.

Once they were in the oven and the timer had been set,

Sara Maria went into organizational mode. She removed everything from the kitchen cabinets, scrubbed them down, then began reorganizing the contents according to some internal schematic.

After watching for a few minutes, Rosie said, "If you're okay here, I have some emails to answer." Two had come in from her brother while Sara Maria was putting the finishing touches on her pies. She was anxious to see if Daniel liked the scene she'd sent him yesterday.

"Sure." Sara Maria didn't even pause to look at her.

"Okay, well I'll be down the hall if you need me."

In the other room Rosie settled on the sofa with her laptop and quickly opened her email account. In his first message Daniel enthused over her scene in gratifying detail. In the next email, however, he asked her to make a bit of a change to fit in an idea he'd had for a new plot twist.

Assuming the change wouldn't take long, Rosie opened her screenplay document. Soon she was so immersed she barely registered the sound of the oven timer going off. Sometime after that Sara Maria interrupted her.

"Um… Rosie? The pies are out of the oven."

Crap. She'd forgotten all about Sara Maria and the pies. Hurriedly she saved and closed her document and then rushed to the kitchen with Brant's sister following behind her.

Rosie found five perfectly golden pies resting on racks to cool. The room was filled with the heavenly aroma of fruit and pastry.

"Wow, they look beautiful. I can't wait to have a taste. Should I make some coffee? I think pie and coffee are one of those perfect combinations... you know, like honey and peanut butter."

"I don't want any."

"No coffee? Would you rather have tea with your pie?"

"I don't want coffee or tea or pie."

"Are you worried about spoiling your dinner?" Speaking of which, Rosie noted, it was definitely time to get Sara Maria back to the care home for hers.

"I don't like to eat pie. Only to bake it."

"Seriously? You don't like pie? And you just baked *five?*" Rosie started to laugh, and then Sara Maria joined in, at which point Huck started to bark, and so no one heard the knock on the back door.

Or the door opening and a voice calling out, "Anybody home?"

And then the voice drawing nearer. "Okay, someone's definitely home. And having a hell of a lot of fun, sounds like."

Chapter Nine

ROSIE HADN'T EXPECTED to see Brant for another couple of hours. His sudden appearance in the intimacy of her kitchen, his masculinity conspicuous against the backdrop of her mother's floral wallpaper, was incredibly distracting.

He was in jeans and a navy work shirt with the sleeves rolled up. Without the restraint of his hat, his dark hair curled at his forehead, around his ears and against the collar of his shirt, in a boyishly appealing manner.

Rosie's pulse raced and she automatically patted down her hair, trying to remember if she'd bothered with mascara this morning.

"I tried knocking but no one answered."

"I guess we were laughing too hard to hear you." Rosie glanced from Brant to his sister, who had immediately sobered at his arrival.

"I can't remember when I last heard Sara Maria sound so happy."

"We were breaking up over the fact that she doesn't like pies—and she just baked five." Rosie smiled and expected

Brant to do the same, but oddly he frowned instead.

"You mean with your help, right?"

"Not really. Sara Maria did it all. I just sat here and watched. Well, for most of the time I watched."

"I told you I know how to bake pies," Sara Maria said self-righteously to her brother.

"Yeah and you also told me you could drive, then damn near killed us by running into a tree."

Sara Maria's gaze dropped and her skin flushed a hot red. "I got nervous when you yelled at me."

"I didn't yell the first two times I told you to hit the brakes."

"Time out," Rosie said, quickly. "I'm surprised to see you so early, Brant. I thought you had to work until six."

Sara Maria crossed her arms over her chest and glowered at her brother as he took a deep breath, obviously reining in his temper.

He answered Rosie tersely. "Boss let us off early because of the rain. I admit I figured it would be good to check how you were making out. I hope you were careful with the oven? Sara Maria shouldn't be using one without supervision."

"Well, when I wasn't right here, I was in the very next room."

"You left her alone in the kitchen?"

"Only for half an hour or so." Not that long, but still Rosie felt a little sheepish knowing how completely she'd forgotten about Sara Maria during that time.

"Mom let me bake whenever I wanted."

"Sure. With her help."

"That's not true," Sara Maria's eyes flashed with anger and tears. "You always act like I'm a baby, but I'm not."

Rosie held her breath, wondering if they were in for one of the infamous tantrums but Sara Maria didn't fall to the floor or start wailing. Instead, she brushed past her brother, heading for the door.

"I'm going back to the home. It's where you think I belong anyway."

Brant was about to follow her, when Rosie caught his arm. "Hang on. I think you should let her go."

"Are you crazy?"

"If you follow after her now, you'll end up wounding her sense of pride even more than you already have." She studied his face, but saw no sign of remorse for the way he'd spoken to his sister.

"Her safety is more important than her self-pride."

What a stubborn man. Did he really believe Sara Maria wasn't capable of walking four blocks? Rosie studied his eyes and could only see sincerity. "We can call the care home and ask them to watch for her. If she doesn't arrive in ten minutes we'll both go out looking for her. Do you have the number?"

Brant took a few moments to consider her words, then pulled out his phone and made the connection.

"Hello, this is Brant Willington. My sister is on her way

to you right now. She should be there momentarily. Could you give me a call back when she—"

He paused as the person on the other end of the line spoke for a few moments.

"So you can see her?"

More speaking from the other end, and finally Brant's shoulders relaxed.

"Good. Thanks a lot." He slipped his phone back into his pocket, then turned to Rosie with his brow furrowed. "You think I'm too protective, but I assure you I'm not."

"I don't mean to judge. But you have to admit you took the wind out of her sails when you jumped on her just now."

"Is that how you see the situation?"

"You said yourself you hadn't seen your sister laugh in a long time. And ten minutes after you show up, she's in a huff and running out the door."

Brant's jaw tightened. "Baking a few pies doesn't make Sara Maria a responsible adult. You have no idea, Rosie. Just last year my sister, mom, and I were out for pizza, when Sara Maria looked out the window and saw a woman walking a border collie puppy. Before I knew it, she'd jumped out of her chair and rushed outside to pet the puppy."

"Okay, that's a little impulsive. But what's the harm in in?"

"The woman was on the other side of the street. My sister didn't even stop to check for cars. She just ran and she was nearly hit by a truck. The driver slammed on his brakes so hard he set off his own air bag."

Rosie felt humbled. "Okay. I'm sorry. I can see now why you freaked out about her walking home alone. But isn't it possible she learned from that experience?"

"Maybe. But I can't predict what crazy thing she might do next time. Like I told you, my sister lives in her own world."

Rosie didn't know what to say. She had no basis to challenge what Brant was saying, other than her own observations which told her Sara Maria was higher functioning than her brother gave her credit for.

"Did your sister have to go to a special needs school?"

"Academically, she's smart. Very smart. It's her common sense that's lacking. After Dad split and we moved to Montana, I had to babysit her a lot and, believe me, it wasn't easy keeping her safe, especially once she was old enough to start baking. She wasn't supposed to even go in the kitchen when Mom wasn't home, but I can't tell you how many times she set off the smoke alarm. Luckily I was there before things got out of hand."

"Sounds like you had a lot of responsibility. And not much time for after school sports or hanging out with friends."

He waved that off. "I had no friends anyway. It was a tough age to move from an urban school in Chicago to one in the middle of ranching country. I didn't fit in at all, not until my mom enrolled me in riding and roping lessons the summer after my junior year."

"My family lived in Marietta all my life. I've never had to try and fit in at a new school, but I'm sure I wouldn't have enjoyed the experience much." It would have been especially difficult for Brant given that he had to look after his autistic sister all the time.

"The worst was missing my dad. We'd been close, but after the move I hardly saw him."

"He didn't fly you back to Chicago for visits?"

"He couldn't handle Sara Maria. And I guess he figured it wasn't fair to spend time with one kid and not the other." Brant shook his head. "Hang on. I never meant to start complaining. And I sure as hell don't want your sympathy. I just want to make sure Sara Maria doesn't con you into believing she's more capable than she really is. There's a reason I put her in that home. It's not like I wanted to do it."

Rosie nodded, but couldn't help wondering if Brant was being totally honest with himself about that.

ROSIE'S TOFFEE-COLORED EYES were warm with sympathy, but Brant could see approbation, too. Obviously she felt he'd been too hard on his sister. What did she know about being the older sibling to a sister with special needs?

He had no need to justify himself here. While he was far from a saint, he was a decent guy. He worked hard, treated people honestly, and tried to do right by his sister.

If Rosie couldn't see that, well that was her problem.

"I ought to get to work now. I brought some lumber to fix the rotten boards on your porch."

That earned him a smile, at least, albeit a small one.

"Thank you. Can I help?"

Soft curls had escaped her ponytail and framed her slightly flushed, round face. She was standing with one hand on the curve of her waist and her legs seemed to go on forever. Even though he was annoyed with her, he still found her appealing.

Which pissed him off. He preferred to be attracted to women who thought he was pretty much perfect the way he was.

"You can pick out colors for the house exterior and trim. I brought samples with me."

Without another word he strode outside to grab them from his truck. When he returned, she was at the sink, peeling vegetables, standing in a position that made it impossible for him not to notice what a cute rear end she had.

He dropped the samples on the table, maybe a little more forcibly than necessary, since the smacking noise caused her to jump.

"Just write down the colors you want and next time I come I'll start painting."

She turned around, wiping her hands on a towel. "Are you annoyed with me?" She studied his face. "Still mad about my comments on the way you spoke to your sister?"

He shrugged. "I've moved on. Now let me get to those steps while I've still got plenty of light."

She said nothing to that. Fine. It wasn't as if he'd expected an apology.

Outside, he pried his crowbar into the space between two rotten boards and gave a good push. The wood cracked loudly and splinters flew up in the air.

Guess he'd used a little more force than necessary.

Gradually his work calmed him down. Though he loved training horses best, his second favorite job was building things. Something on the ranch was always in need of fixing, whether it was a gate, a fence, or one of the outbuildings.

Last year the boss had commissioned a new horse barn. When the manager of the construction company had realized how talented Brant was with a saw and a nail gun, he'd been assigned to the project full time.

Brant had loved every moment and was incredibly proud of how it had turned out. The barn was state of the art, a perfect marriage of function, practicality, and beauty.

Compared to that project, fixing a few rotten stairs, some window trims and a soft patch on an old porch floor was a cakewalk, but Brant still took a lot of care. No matter how small the job, he was meticulous. As he worked he became aware of delicious cooking smells emanating from the kitchen. His stomach rumbled—his last meal had been six hours ago—but he kept working.

Brant was putting away his tools when Rosie came out the front door about an hour later.

He'd forgotten his resentment, but a sliver of it returned at the sight of her. "Want to inspect my work? Make sure it's up to code?"

She didn't seem to notice the heavy sarcasm in his tone.

"Looks great." She went closer so she could see how perfectly he'd matched the rungs. "Better than new in fact. Thank you."

She glanced at his truck, then back at him. "But I didn't come out here to check on your work. I was wondering if you'd like a bowl of stew before you leave?"

The offer was tempting, especially since he'd been drooling over the cooking smells, wafting from the open kitchen window for the past hour. Plus, it was already seven-thirty and he'd put in a long day.

"Wouldn't want to put you out."

"I made a big batch." She hesitated, gave him a cautious look, then added, "Plus I've got five pies for dessert."

A second ticked by, then another. Finally Brant laughed. He couldn't help it and, as soon as he did, her shoulders relaxed.

With their discord apparently behind them, they went inside and Rosie pointed out the powder room where he could wash up for dinner.

Once he was done, he found Rosie in the kitchen where she'd set out place mats, bowls, and a basket of dinner rolls to go with the stew. The kitchen table was in an alcove overlooking a lawn choked with Virginia creeper and lilac bushes in need of serious pruning.

Following his gaze, Rosie sighed. "Yes, the back yard is looking pretty rough, too, isn't it? Dad was the one with the green thumb. You should have seen how nice it looked back in the days when he had his health."

The combination of sadness and nostalgia on her face brought back the pain of Brant's own recent loss. "We both lost our parents too young."

"Yes. It's easy to take them for granted, isn't it? Until you don't have them, and then you realize how much you needed them."

"Mom was in excellent health up until her car accident."

"That must have made her loss even more of a shock."

Brant nodded. He and his mom had never talked about what would happen to Sara Maria after she died. They'd both assumed they'd have years—decades—to sort that out. Now Brant would have given anything for some of his mother's counsel. But all he had was the advice she'd given him as a kid.

"Watch out for your sister. Keep her safe."

Rosie handed him a ladle. "If you don't mind being casual, how about we serve ourselves straight from the pot on the stove?"

"Works for me." He insisted on letting her go first, then took a generous serving of the chunks of beef, potato, onion and carrot bathed in a caramelized gravy that smelled heavenly.

Just one taste brought back happy memories of weekend dinners when he'd been a child, before Sara Maria decided she was vegetarian.

"This is good. Reminds me of my mom's."

"Thanks, but in the interest of full disclosure you should know there are only about ten recipes I do a decent job of and stew is the top of the list."

That made him chuckle. "You surprise me. I had you pegged as the domesticated kind."

Her gaze shifted to a chair in the corner where she'd stacked a laptop and a rather beaten-looking notebook. Then she cocked her eyebrow in a fashion he was beginning to recognize as politely confrontational.

"Because I'm a woman?"

He saw the need for a quick sidestep. "No. Because you work in the food industry."

Her expression shifted from affronted to amused. "Chocolate isn't *food*."

"Why not? We eat it, don't we?"

"Maybe you do. I savor it. Chocolate…" She paused to search for the right words, "Chocolate is like fine wine or really good coffee. It's about flavor and texture, yes, but it's more than something to eat. Enjoying chocolate should be a full-on, sensory experience."

The sensory experience Brant was experiencing watching

her describe chocolate had nothing to do with food. At all.

He remembered a woman once telling him the perfect human face shape was oval, but watching Rosie, he saw that was wrong. Round faces were much more appealing, especially if they were accompanied with soft, plump, kissable lips and eyes that brought to mind melted toffee.

He wondered what Rosie would say if he told her the way she described chocolate was the way he felt about sex.

Good sense made him decide to hold his tongue.

"Maybe I should come to your chocolate shop more often."

He watched, fascinated, as the corners of her kissable lips turned up in a smile.

"For three months I wondered who you were buying those chocolates for. I never once guessed your sister." A light sparked in her eyes. "That's why you'd never try anything new, right? Because Sara Maria doesn't like change."

He nodded, acknowledging the truth in that. "The first time I bought her chocolates, she was still in the hospital after her breakdown."

"The one she had after your mother's accident?"

"Yeah." Just thinking back to those days made his chest ache. "I'd never seen my sister in such bad shape before. It was awful. Mom was the only one who could help her, but Mom wasn't with us anymore. Out of desperation I decided to try buying her a box of chocolates. Do you remember what you said, the first time I was in your shop?"

"Uh huh. You asked what our most popular chocolate was and I said it was the dark chocolate caramels with Himalayan pink salt."

"Right. So I bought a box and took them to Sara Maria, fully expecting her to ignore both me and the chocolates. But she surprised me by eating one. And then another. And after that she started talking again."

"See? I told you there's something special about chocolate."

Brant wasn't fooled by her little joke. He could see tears sparkling in her eyes. "Every time I visited her after that, I brought her another box of chocolates."

"I'm sorry I ever tried to get you to buy anything else." Rosie tilted her head as she regarded him thoughtfully. "You really care about your sister."

"Of course I do."

"I'm sorry I accused you of being heavy-handed. But I do wonder if Sara Maria belongs in the May Bell Care Home. I know some of the employees who work there and they're lovely, kind people. But it seems to me that most of the other residents are either a lot older or recovering from a serious medical trauma."

She was eyeing him cautiously. Maybe she expected another flare up. But he'd worked off his anger and all that was left was a heavy load of exhaustion. "When Sara Maria was released from the hospital after her breakdown, she was in rough shape. I didn't know where to turn. The care home seemed like the best solution then."

"Now maybe it isn't?"

"Yeah, that's what they're telling me—but what are my options?"

"There's got to be some other place."

"Trust me, I've looked. There isn't."

Rosie stared at him, wondering if he was avoiding the obvious, or if he truly didn't see it. Surely the best place for his sister would be living with him.

Chapter Ten

BRANT HAD BEEN gone for twenty minutes when Portia came home around eight-thirty that evening, using the front door and walking straight into the living room. As soon as Rosie heard footsteps on the porch, she automatically saved and closed the document she'd been working on.

"Hey, Rosie." Portia paused to hang up her jacket and set down her purse and a plastic shopping bag. "How was your evening? I see someone fixed the porch. Was it Brant?"

The neat ponytail Portia had worn to work that morning was barely hanging in there. Not only was her hair a mess, but she had faint smudges under her eyes and her smile looked both fake and weak.

"Are you okay? Did Sage make you work this late?"

"No. I went for a walk after work. A long walk."

Rosie was concerned, but didn't want to nag. "If you're hungry we've got stew. And rhubarb raspberry pie."

"Did you say pie?" Portia perked up and headed to the kitchen. Rosie set aside her laptop and followed.

"Wow, you weren't kidding when you said we had pie."

Although Rosie had convinced Brant to take one home to share with his bunkmates, four picture-perfect pies remained on the kitchen counter, one missing a couple slices.

"Turns out Sara Maria loves to bake."

"These look gorgeous. I've made lots of pies with my mom and ours never turn out like this. Do they taste as good as they look?"

"You may find this hard to believe but they actually taste *better* than they look."

"Okay. I'm going in." Portia grabbed a plate and a knife and cut herself a slice even more slender than the sliver Rosie had eaten after her stew.

As Portia pressed the side of the fork into the pie for her first bite, the pastry flaked around the thick, lusciously red fruit. Carefully Portia raised the fork to her mouth. A moment later her eyes widened. She chewed very, very slowly, then swallowed and let out a sigh.

"What the heck is in there? There's got to be some kind of secret ingredient."

"I watched her bake them. No secret ingredients. At least none that I saw."

Portia's gaze swept around the kitchen and paused at the two bowls sitting in the drying rack.

"So did Sara Maria stay for dinner?"

"No. Brant grabbed a quick bite after he fixed the stairs."

"A quick bite of what?" Portia teased.

"Oh, stop it. We did have a good talk, though. He's really mixed-up about his sister. He's so preoccupied with keeping her safe he's stuck her in that home where she doesn't fit in. Sara Maria is suffocating."

"Anyone who can bake a pie like this shouldn't be in a care home," Portia agreed.

Rosie noticed that despite her admiration for the pie, Portia hadn't taken a second bite.

Leaving her plate on the counter, Portia went to the fridge. Her hand went from the pitcher of water, to the gallon of almond milk, then back to the water. She poured herself a tall glass and drank half of it.

"I hate to sound like your mom, but did you have any dinner tonight?"

"Please don't quiz me, Rosie."

Rosie wanted to respect her wishes, but in the short while she'd known Portia, the other woman hadn't eaten a proper meal. She hoped her new friend didn't have an eating disorder. "Just tell me you normally eat more than the bits of salad and bread I've seen you nibble on since I met you."

"Trust me, I do. A month ago, if you'd put that pie in front of me, I probably would have devoured two pieces already."

"So why not now?" Rosie persisted.

Portia turned her back to the fridge and sagged against it. "I haven't been feeling well for almost a month."

Rosie hadn't expected this answer and was immediately worried. "Have you been to the doctor?"

"I hoped it was just a virus and I'd be better soon."

But she obviously wasn't. "I really like my GP. Want me to send you her contact information?"

"Yeah. That's probably a good idea." Portia left the room and returned a moment later with the plastic shopping bag she'd left at the front door. "There is one more explanation for how I'm feeling that I need to rule out."

In that instant, Rosie knew what was inside the shopping bag.

Knew, too, what Portia needed to find out.

"You think you could be pregnant?"

Portia stared at her for a long moment. "It's possible."

No one spoke for a few minutes. Dozens of questions popped into Rosie's mind. Most of all, she wondered if Portia's ex-boyfriend was the potential father, and if this was the reason Portia had dropped out of college.

But Portia wouldn't want an inquisition. Rosie took a deep breath, then crossed the room, took Portia's hand and gave it a squeeze. "You ready to find out?"

After another hesitation, Portia nodded.

"Okay." Rosie went down the hall and opened the door to the powder room. It was hard to believe that less than three hours ago Brant had been in here, washing his hands. Their dinner together felt so long ago now.

As Portia stepped into the bathroom, Rosie said, "I'll wait out here. Call me if... if you need anything."

The process took all of two minutes. Rosie waited in anguish, not sure what outcome to even hope for. When Portia emerged with a plastic stick in her hand, Rosie didn't have to examine it to know the verdict. She could tell by the paleness of Portia's skin. The fear in her eyes.

"It's positive," she finally said. "I'm going to have a baby."

And for the second time since Rosie had met her, Portia dissolved into tears.

IN A SHOW of solidarity, Rosie stayed up until almost midnight with Portia. Since Portia wasn't ready to talk, they decided to watch a movie. Rosie suggested one of her favorites, *500 Days of Summer.*

"Haven't seen it. What's it about?" Portia settled into the corner of the sofa, pulling the throw Rosie's mother had knitted up to her chest.

"It's about love, but it isn't a love story. I once saw it on a list of movies to make you glad that you're single."

Portia laughed. "You're so awesome. It sounds perfect."

As the movie played, Rosie had to struggle to keep her mouth shut. In her family it was normal to analyze the turning points and character development in a movie, to discuss why the director might have decided to shoot a scene a certain way, or chosen a specific backdrop for a close-up.

This had driven their mother crazy, sometimes she'd insisted she wouldn't watch a show with them unless they all promised to keep their ideas and opinions to themselves. On the odd occasions when they managed to do so, as soon as the credits started rolling, their words would come spilling out.

When the movie ended, Rosie was anxious to hear what Portia had thought. "Did you like it?"

"Sort of. To be honest, I had trouble concentrating." Portia sighed as she stood up. "Thanks for keeping me company. It was nice not to be alone. I'm going to try and sleep now."

Rosie hugged her friend then went to bed as well, but though she was extremely tired, sleep didn't come easily. She couldn't help brooding about Portia's pregnancy and Sara Maria's unhappiness, and whether her house would finally sell. Almost more disturbing than these worries were her thoughts of Brant. His attitude toward his sister was so frustrating. It should have made her like him less, but oddly the opposite was true. Maybe because she sensed his cluelessness stemmed, not so much from a lack of caring, but from some sort of blind spot.

When Rosie woke at eight the next morning, Portia was asleep, but there were signs she'd been up a good portion of the night. A stack of clean laundry was folded on one of the kitchen chairs and a dozen freshly baked apple oatmeal muffins were on the counter, along with a note.

Didn't sleep much last night. Hope doing my laundry and baking these muffins didn't disturb you. I've sent

Aunt Sage a text explaining I won't be at work today.
I'm going to try and get in to see your doctor.

As she read the note, Rosie gobbled one of the muffins, which was absolutely delicious—moist and full of apple and cinnamon flavors. She considered putting on a pot of coffee, but now that Portia was finally getting some much needed rest she didn't want to risk waking her.

Maybe she'd go to the Java Café for her morning fix. On her way she could drop off the pies at the care home. Sara Maria said she didn't like pie, but surely the other residents and the staff would love them. Rosie covered three pies in plastic wrap, then placed them in a large shallow box. With her purse slung over her shoulder, she quietly let herself out the back door and placed the pies in the trunk of her car.

Marietta was so small, Rosie seldom felt the need to drive, but with all these pies to carry, today it was a necessity. The autumn morning was sunny and warm, and Rosie had to stop at one intersection as a mom and three children hurried by on their way to school. A block further a dog walker strolled by with three dogs on leash, headed for the path along the river, probably.

It was just an average morning in Marietta, but for some reason, today, Rosie saw so much beauty in the mundane. She realized, regardless of the long winter, she was going to miss this place terribly when she moved.

At the care home, the kitchen staff was happy to accept the gift of the pies, though they insisted two was plenty.

Rosie was on her way back to her car with the unwanted third pie when she noticed Sara Maria sitting in a far corner of the lounge area, reading a book.

Instinctively Rosie went over to say hello, but Sara Maria just glanced at her without returning the greeting. Was she upset? Or was this just another of her quirks?

Up close Rosie was able to make out the title of her book, *The Complete Works of Immanuel Kant.*

"Wow, that's heavy stuff."

Gaze still fixed to the printed page Sara Maria said, "He's a German philosopher."

"Um, yeah, I know. But why are you reading his book?" Rosie couldn't imagine doing so, unless it was required material for some course she had to take.

Sara Maria heaved out a breath, then settled the book face down on her lap. "Look around me. I have to do something to keep my sanity."

Rosie did look. She saw a motley collection of men and women, all of whom were decades older than Sara Maria. Some were watching television, others were staring off into space or had their eyes closed, presumably napping already even though it wasn't yet nine in the morning.

"Those two women in the corner by the window are playing Scrabble." Rosie pointed out.

"Yes, I joined in their game once. They wouldn't accept that the word 'oxygen' takes the letter 's' even though I showed them the word right in the Scrabble Dictionary."

"Oh." Rosie studied Sara Maria's face closely, realizing she'd underestimated her intellectual ability. By far. "Does Brant know you read books like that?" She pointed to the one on Sara Maria's lap.

"Brant knows I like to read. Our mother used to take us to the library every week when we were kids. But he probably isn't aware of my interest in philosophy. It started when my mother bought me *Sophie's World* for my sixteenth birthday. I was frustrated by the blend of fiction and fact and wanted to read the works of the philosophers for myself."

"Oh my lord, Sara Maria. You *so* don't belong in this place."

Sara Maria gave her a look that basically implied, *duh.*

"I'm going to talk to your brother about this," Rosie promised, not mentioning she'd already broached the topic without much success. She simply *had* to find a better place for Sara Maria to live.

"Don't bother. My brother wants me someplace where he doesn't have to worry about me. The care home suits him perfectly."

"Don't you think he loves you? That he wants you to be happy?"

Sara Maria considered the question for a while before answering. "You have to know a person before you can love them."

"And you don't think Brant knows you?"

"I'm just his weird kid sister. Someone he's had to look

after all his life. I don't blame him for being sick of it. As long as I'm in this place, he gets to live his life the way he wants. At least most of the time."

"But he does care. He visits you every Friday."

"It's just an obligation. He doesn't like doing it."

Rosie suspected there was at least a kernel of truth in what Sara Maria was saying, but she couldn't accept it all. "Maybe he feels that way a little sometimes. But I'm positive he loves you."

She could tell Sara Maria didn't believe her and she longed to give the younger woman a hug, or at least put a hand on her shoulder, but she didn't dare. "I bet you feel super lonesome without your mom. I really miss my parents, too. Part of moving on after you've lost someone though, is meeting new people. Making new friends. I think you need to do that."

To her surprise Sara Maria seemed open to the idea.

"How do I do that? Make friends?"

"Well... there's me, right? We're in the process of becoming friends." Even as she said this, though, she felt a ping of guilt, knowing she would be moving soon.

But Sara Maria either didn't know about the impending move or didn't care. A soft light shone in her eyes. Her lips turned up into a tiny smile. "Yes. Thank you, Rosie. You're right, it is good to have a friend."

ROSIE STOPPED INTO the Java Café to buy a large latte before making her way to Copper Mountain Chocolates. She'd had an idea and she wanted input from Dakota and Sage.

Business was bustling for so early in the morning. Dakota had three customers lined up at the till, one of whom was Rosie's chocolate-addicted realtor, Maddie Cash. Rosie stopped to chat for a moment. As she and Maddie rhapsodized about the joys of Sage's hot chocolate, Rosie noticed Dakota was looking brighter-faced these days. Hopefully it was a sign she was getting over her rough breakup with her long-term boyfriend Craig Wilkins.

When she finally slipped back into the kitchen, Rosie found Sage pouring a vat of melted dark chocolate over a huge tray of dried, tart cherries, grated coconut, and chopped hazelnuts. Yum, Sage was making one of Rosie's favorites.

Rosie set the pie down on a free corner by the sink, then watched as Sage layered the velvety chocolate over the fruit and nut mixture. After scraping the pot clean Sage then used a pastry spatula to smooth the chocolate evenly over the entire tray.

"That looks almost as good as I know it's going to taste."

Sage smiled briefly. "Is that why you dropped in on your day off? To grab some fresh cherry hazelnut bark? If so, there's a tray cooling in the second refrigerator."

"Thanks, but I actually want you to taste something for me this time."

As Sage looked up, a strand of her red hair fell into her

eyes. Using the back of her hand, she swept it away. "Is that a pie you came in with?"

"Yes. It wasn't baked by me, you'll be relieved to hear."

Again Sage smiled.

"I've been hanging out with the autistic sister of one of our regular customers. Her name is Sara Maria. She has some issues that affect her ability to live independently, but she's really smart and she's also an awesome baker. I wondered if maybe we could help her become more independent by finding a place where she could sell her pies."

The beginnings of a worried frown appeared on her face. "I hope you weren't thinking of here."

"No," Rosie quickly reassured her. "But maybe Rachel would take them at the Gingerbread and Dessert Factory?"

"Hm. Are you sure the pie is good enough? Rachel's standards are very high."

"I think so. But I want your opinion and Dakota's, too. May I cut a few slices?"

"Sure." Sage transferred the tray to the fridge, then went to wash her hands. When she was finished she asked, "So how is Portia this morning? I was worried when I got her message last night."

"Oh, still under the weather." Rosie was glad she could keep her gaze lowered to the pie. She'd always been bad at lying, even white lies or lies of omission.

"Poor thing, getting sick when she's already dealing with so much. She's such a sweetie. I hate to see her so unhappy."

Not knowing what to say, Rosie made a murmur of agreement.

"Does she talk to you, Rosie?" Sage asked abruptly. Then immediately she apologized. "I shouldn't pry. It's just I can't help worrying about her."

"We talk some," Rosie said vaguely.

"Well, I'm glad you took her in as a roommate. Portia obviously needs some space from her family right now, but I wouldn't want her to be alone."

"It's been nice for me, too."

Sage gave her arm a sympathetic squeeze. "Have you had any offers on your house?"

"No. But I have someone working on repairs and new paint. The guy with the autistic sister. Hopefully that will help." Rosie quickly handed Sage one of the servings of pie, hoping to distract her from asking any questions about said guy, questions she wasn't ready to answer, given her confused state of mind about Brant Willington.

Sage took her first bite. It was almost comical watching her reaction. She chewed slowly, with obvious relish, before finally swallowing.

"That pie is fantastic."

They called Dakota into the kitchen next and let her have a sample. Dakota quickly came to the same conclusion.

"It's awesome. Can you save the rest of this so I can enjoy it when I have time for a proper break?"

Since the bell had just sounded, signaling a new customer, Dakota relinquished her fork with reluctance and went back to work.

"I'm finished here for the day and I'm not needed at home for another hour." Sage had devoured her slice already and was wrapping the remaining pie back in the plastic. "Let me take this to Rachel so she can have a sample. I haven't seen her in ages and this will give me an excuse to pay her a visit."

Rosie had just noticed an incoming message from her brother. Generally this meant he had a new scene for her to work on, so she was glad to take Sage up on her offer. "You'll let me know what she says?"

"I will, and I'm betting the answer will be positive. Pie this good will sell itself."

BACK IN HER car, Rosie read the message from Daniel. As she'd suspected he had the next scene of his pilot episode ready for her. This time he'd merely mapped out the scene structure and left her to fill in the details, especially the dialogue.

In his message he asked if she could get this back to him before tomorrow morning. She typed back. *That's not much time but I'll try."*

At home, Rosie used the back entrance, hoping to find the house quiet so she could get straight to work, but Portia was at the kitchen table in front of her open laptop, jotting notes. She had her hair in a messy bun and was wearing flannel pajama bottoms decorated with puppies and an oversized pink t-shirt.

Her color was good, and she seemed perky, which was a big improvement from the previous night.

"Hey, how are you doing?"

"Better, thanks. Sorry about last night."

"No problem." Rosie hesitated, wondering if Portia wanted to discuss her pregnancy, but Portia's next words were on an entirely different subject.

"I've been working on our chocolate and wine tasting event. Got a minute to talk about it?"

Rosie supposed she could put off her writing for a little while. "Sure."

Portia flipped back a few pages in the notebook. "I called the Two Old Goats wine store on Front Street and told them about our idea."

"And were they interested?"

"I spoke to Clifford. He said it sounded like a winning idea. And he had a brilliant suggestion—why don't we host the event on Halloween and have everyone dress in costumes?"

Rosie grinned. "Love it!"

"So fun, right? I've been jotting down some possible names for the event. What do you think of *Dark Magic Chocolate & Wine Tasting*?

"It's good. Dark magic works for Halloween and it also makes me think of Sage's delicious single origin dark chocolate bars."

Portia smiled. "I'm so glad you like it. I have some rudimentary graphic design skills so I was going to create a poster for the store. I also thought we could email out invitations to our customers."

"I'm afraid we don't have an email listing of our customers. I've been encouraging Sage to start one."

"Oh, boy. When it comes to marketing, we're really starting from scratch aren't we?"

"Last Christmas I tried to convince her to have a contest for a huge chocolate gift basket. To enter people would have to give us their names and email addresses, and permission to add them to our customer list. She wouldn't go for it. Said it was too pushy."

Portia groaned. "Oh, Aunt Sage. Really?"

"We'll both have to work on her."

"I know. I'll set up a meeting at the wine store and we'll ambush her. Clifford told me that he and his partner have over five hundred names on their email list." Portia closed her lap top and got up from the table. "I better get a move on."

"Are you going into work for the afternoon?"

"No. Your doctor squeezed me in with an eleven forty-five appointment. I'm going to take a quick shower first."

"Oh. Good. I'm glad you got in so quickly."

"Yeah. I think I suspected this for a while now. I have to stop living in denial and face facts."

"Is this why you dropped out of college? Because you figured you might be pregnant?"

Portia sighed. "Not really. But it does stem from the main problem."

Before Rosie could ask what she meant, Portia had left the room. Rosie replayed her parting words but couldn't make sense of them. It seemed as if Portia thought she had a problem bigger than being pregnant. But how was that possible?

Chapter Eleven

A S THE TOWN of Marietta came into view, Brant reflect-ed on how dramatically his life had shifted recently. Not more than a week ago, the sight of this town had filled him with the urge to pull his truck around and speed back to the Three Bars Ranch.

But today he was looking forward to his arrival.

The reason for his about-face was obvious.

Rosie.

She confounded him and challenged him, but she'd also cast some sort of sweet spell over him. Last night when they'd eaten dinner together he'd thought what a nice change it made from having dinner with the guys at the bunkhouse. Later, when he was trying to sleep in the narrow bed that had suited him just fine for the past ten years, he'd found himself wondering what it would be like to sleep with Rosie beside him.

It wasn't just the sex, though he imagined that would be great.

It was the cuddling after. The warmth of another body

beside him all night long. And waking up to feminine curves and a sweet smile, instead of three unshaven men, grouchy as bears before their first morning coffee.

These kinds of thoughts were dangerous.

When he'd graduated from high school, the job at Three Bars Ranch had suited him perfectly. He'd brushed aside his mother's suggestion he go to college. He liked reading, but wasn't fond of other scholarly pursuits. He wanted a job that kept him active and allowed him to spend time outdoors, not cooped up in some office.

Guys had come and gone from the bunkhouse in the ten years he'd worked for Pete Proctor. A few had been jerks but, for the most part, his fellow ranch hands were good to work beside during the day and fun to drink beer with at night. Friday nights spent chatting up the women and dancing at one of the local bars was enough social life for his taste.

But his tastes were changing.

Much as he loved his job hanging out with the guys and living in the bunkhouse was getting old.

He wasn't sure what had spurred the shift in his thinking. His mother dying. His new responsibility for his sister. Or meeting Rosie.

Then again, maybe it was none of the above, but simply a function of aging. Maturing. In another year he'd be thirty. It was an age that made a man take stock. He had no house, no degree, no special woman in his life. Hell, half the guys he'd gone to school with were fathers already.

At least he had some money socked away. He wasn't a big spender and most of what he made went straight into savings.

As he whizzed by the sign welcoming him to Marietta, Brant lowered his speed, then headed to the Big Z Hardware to pick up the paint he'd ordered by phone during his lunch hour. The owner, Paul Zabrinski, helped him carry the gallons to his truck, complimenting him on the choice of colors.

"Not my doing. That was what the customer wanted."

"And who would that be?" Paul asked, handing over the last gallon can.

"Rosie Linn. She works at the chocolate shop."

"Ah, Rosie. Good of her to stay and look after her father the way she did. Her older brother's some sort of big time screenwriter in L.A. they say. Must take after his father."

"How so?"

"Brams Linn wrote bestselling thrillers. I've read a bunch of them. My dad is a big fan. Owns the entire collection." Paul offered his hand. "Thanks for your business. Hope the house turns out well. Let me know if you have any problems with the paint."

Five minutes later, Brant pulled up at Rosie's tired-looking house, parking in the lane beside her detached garage. Before knocking on the back door, he ran his fingers over the kitchen window frame. Paint flecked off in his hands.

He shifted his gaze upward, and was surprised to see Rosie looking back at him. She was sitting at the kitchen table and had obviously been working at something on her laptop, but the moment she spotted him she slapped it shut.

"Come on in," she called out.

The screen door was unlocked, just like yesterday. He paused at the entrance to the kitchen, trying to figure out why she looked different. And then it hit him—she was wearing glasses. They looked geeky, but in a cute way.

"Like the librarian look. Very sexy."

She whipped them off, and somehow the clip that had been holding back her hair snapped off at the same time, sending her curls bouncing down to her shoulders.

"Good," he said. "Now toss your head back. Wish I had a camera."

"Oh, stop it."

To his great disappointment, she snagged the clip from where it had fallen to the floor and refastened it in her hair. "I can't believe it's after six already."

"Just thought I'd check in before I started scraping. Didn't mean to interrupt your... whatever you were doing." He glanced at her laptop and the notepad beside it.

She didn't explain, just pushed both to the far end of the table. "I've never prepped a house for painting before, but if you show me what to do, I can help."

"It's not rocket science. You just scrape away as much loose paint as you can. The idea is to have a smooth service for applying the new paint."

"That makes sense." She picked up her phone, scrolled, then frowned. "I was just wondering where my new roommate is. Apparently she's invited to a barbecue at her family's ranch."

So it would be just the two of them. He wasn't sorry to hear that.

Turned out Rosie was no slouch when it came to physical work and she managed to look damn cute while she was doing it.

Brant paused often to watch her and had to keep reminding himself he was here to work. He'd always thought she was cute, but lately he could not keep his eyes off her.

She had a way about her that grew on a man. And though she didn't dress to flaunt her figure, she sure had a great one.

By seven-thirty it was too dark to keep working.

"I'll come by tomorrow to finish this up," he said as he folded up the ladder. "Should be able to start painting this weekend. According to the forecast the weather's going to cooperate." It was supposed to stay warm and dry for the next fourteen days, but beyond that, he knew they couldn't count on anything. This part of Montana was usually hit with a hard frost before Halloween.

"I'm excited to see this old place get a fresh coat of paint. She sure needs it." Rosie brushed paint flecks off her jeans. "Hungry? There's stew leftover from last night if you're not picky."

It was just the invitation he'd been waiting for. "As it happens, I have a merlot in my truck that might pair well with that."

She did a double take. "Marvelous. I'll get out the white linens shall I?"

By the time he'd stowed the ladder and retrieved the wine, Rosie had the stew in the microwave and was setting out bowls. She glanced at the bottle in his hand.

"Oh, you really do have wine. I thought you were joking."

"I have to admit I hoped I'd get invited to dinner again."

"Stew was that good, was it?"

"Stew was fine. The company was even better."

For a moment their glances held. Then she opened a drawer and tossed him a corkscrew. "Glasses are in the cupboard over the microwave."

During the meal they talked about the other repairs needed at her house, and then Rosie asked him if he knew Sara Maria read college level books about philosophy.

"No, but it doesn't surprise me. She was always good at school, though Mom had to go to bat for her every year to get her teachers to accept her in their classrooms and work around her idiosyncrasies. When she graduated last year, Mom hoped she'd apply to college. She had the marks for a full scholarship."

"Why didn't she?"

"The idea of college just seemed too big to her I guess. And Mom was probably too tired to push it. Getting Sara Maria through regular school was hard enough."

"Sounds like your mom was pretty special."

"She was." When they were both finished eating, he got up to clear the table. "And so was your dad, I hear. The owner of the hardware store was telling me your dad was a bestselling novelist."

"It's true."

"That's impressive. Do you have any of his books?"

"Of course. They're in my parents' bedroom. My dad did all his writing there. Want to see?"

She was obviously proud of her father, which was kind of adorable.

"I do."

He followed her down the hall to the spacious master bedroom. The spotless room had a museum-type aura about it, no doubt because it hadn't been lived in for many months. Brant's attention went first to the bed, pristinely made, with a folded quilt at the edge. Rosie walked past this, to the far corner where a large desk was flanked by a filing cabinet and a bookshelf.

First thing he noticed was a portrait of a happy-looking couple in their fifties. The woman had the same round face as Rosie, the man was clearly overweight and had kind, brown eyes. "These your parents?"

"Yes. They had that photo taken shortly after my mom's

cancer diagnosis."

"They were older then, your parents?"

"Mom was almost thirty when she had Daniel, and forty-one with me."

"There's a big gap between Sara Maria and me, too."

"Not the easiest way to have a family. I was only six when Daniel moved out of the house. I hardly knew him until Mom got sick. After that he was a lot better about phoning regularly. And he came home every Thanksgiving and Christmas."

Brant nodded, but made no comment about there being a lot of days in the year between Christmas and Thanksgiving. During that time he supposed Rosie had shouldered the brunt of the care for their parents.

"And here are the books." Rosie pointed to a row of mass market paperbacks on the lower shelf. "All twenty-two novels, in order of publication."

"Impressive." He opened one at random and read the dedication, which was to "my son Daniel Linn, the screenwriter."

"Sounds like your dad was pretty proud of your brother."

"We all were. And I still am, of course. He's working on an idea for TV series right now. If it gets backing, it will really make his career."

"Sounds exciting. Guess you can't wait to move there and be a part of it?"

She nodded.

"It's good to have dreams."

"Do you?"

He focused on Rosie. She was so easy to talk to. And so pretty. It was a wonder the men of Marietta weren't lined up at her door. "I'm more about living for the moment."

"Is that a fact?"

He nodded.

They were standing so close, their shoulders just inches apart. He could see sandy-colored freckles on her nose, and the sweep of her eyelashes as she glanced from him to the bookshelf.

He reached out to touch her hair, which was trying to escape her hair clasp again. "I think this is about to fall out." Indeed as soon as he touched it, the plastic clip fell to the floor and curls tumbled thickly around her sweet, round face.

Her gaze locked in on his and her pink lips parted.

Maybe it wasn't the smartest idea in the world. But he had to kiss her.

Gently sliding one hand around her waist, brushing the back of her head with the other, he pressed his lips to hers.

For several intoxicating seconds all thoughts were swept from his mind.

Then he felt her hand on his chest. A soft push away.

"What's wrong?"

"This isn't a good idea. We have a deal. We're... business partners."

"That's one way to look at our situation. Here's another.

We're two friends doing favors for one another."

"A week ago you barely knew my name."

"*New* friends then. And you know what happens to men and women who become friends? They often turn into lovers. It happens every day."

"But—I'm going to be moving."

"You're here now. Let me ask you this—did you like the kiss?"

Eyes luminous, she nodded.

"Then how about we try it again?"

ROSIE WOULD HAVE been happy to kiss Brant all night long but when the back door opened and she heard her new roommate call out hello, the mood was broken. As they pulled apart, she stared into his eyes.

"Reality check. Did this really happen?"

His smile was slow but assured. "Yup. And it's damn sure going to happen again."

He was so cocky. She ought to set him down a notch. But why? She'd finally kissed her cowboy and it had been even more amazing than she'd dreamed. Why shouldn't she kiss him again? Take a page out of his book and try living for the moment.

Might be fun.

Heart skipping with excitement she took his hand and led him out to the living room. Portia had just settled into her favorite corner of the sofa, her mobile tablet in hand.

"Oh." Portia's gaze went from Rosie to Brant, then to their connected hands. "I'm sorry, did I interrupt...?"

"Not a problem. I was just showing Brant my father's books."

"Getting late. I was about to leave anyway." Brant nodded at Portia, and then smiled at Rosie. "Tomorrow?"

She liked the sound of that. "Tomorrow."

"I'll see myself out." He touched her arm one last time before leaving. A few moments later, she heard the door shut behind him.

Portia raised her eyebrows.

"Very interesting. Want to share?"

"We did go into the bedroom to look at dad's books. And then... he kissed me."

Rosie wanted to say it again, to sing the words, to dance around the living room.

A tiny voice cautioned her to be more careful. This was so new. She needed to study her own feelings a bit before she talked about them too much.

"You look head over heels, Rosie. I'm happy for you." Portia's smile couldn't mask the sadness in her eyes, though.

Rosie plopped down on the other end of the sofa. "How did your appointment go with the doctor?"

"Fine." Portia glanced down at her tablet, then sighed. "I like her. We had a long appointment. She said I'm perfectly healthy." Portia swallowed. "And confirmed the fact that I'm pregnant."

The news was as expected, but Rosie suspected Portia had held out hope that somehow the drug store kit had been faulty. Not sure of the right thing to say at that moment, Rosie reached over to squeeze her arm.

"She gave me a referral to a clinic for prenatal classes. And a prescription for multivitamins."

She lifted her head. Tears sparkled in her eyes. "I'm so confused, Rosie. And scared."

Rosie murmured sympathetically. She really had no words of comfort to offer. In Portia's shoes, Rosie would feel exactly the same way.

"I'm only twenty-two years old and my life is a mess. How can I possibly have a baby?"

"The father..." Rosie asked tentatively, wondering if he was someone who could help Portia with this decision.

But Portia shook her head emphatically. "This is my call. I have to figure out what to do on my own."

"Maybe, but you should have support. I'm here and happy to listen. But you should talk to your family, too. One of your aunts or your sister. Your mom."

Portia gave another vehement shake of her head. "I'm not ready for that. So far, you're the only person who knows, Rosie. You have to promise to keep my secret."

Chapter Twelve

T HURSDAY WASN'T A regular work day for Rosie but she was covering a shift for Dakota. As she crept out of her bedroom, she found Portia asleep on the sofa. Her heart ached for her friend when she saw the pile of used tissues on the floor beside Portia. Poor thing must have cried herself to sleep.

Since Portia wasn't on the schedule today, Rosie didn't want to wake her so she tiptoed about the house, feeding Huck and letting him out for his constitutional, then grabbing a muffin and an orange for breakfast, before slipping out the back door to walk to the shop.

As bad as she felt for Portia though, memories of her evening with Brant kept putting a smile on her face. At the shop, when she slipped on her apron and fastened her ponytail, she was reminded of the way Brant had released her hair before he kissed her. He really seemed to like her wild, uncontrollable curls.

Which made her feel a little more kindly disposed to them as well.

Cheerfully, Rosie bustled around the shop preparing for opening. At quarter to ten, Sage arrived, riding her bicycle as she often did when the weather was nice. She waved at Rosie through the front window, then circled around to the rear of the store, where she locked her bike.

Rosie went to the kitchen to talk to her. "Good morning. Did you have a chance to take Rachel that pie yesterday?"

"Sure did." Sage removed her bike helmet and gave her head a slight shake, causing her long braid to swing side-to-side. "Rachel loved it and is sure her customers will, too. She wants to meet with Sara Maria first though and iron out some details."

"That's great. Thanks Sage." The opportunity to feel productive and earn some of her own money would be great for Sara Maria's self-esteem. It would also give her an opportunity to meet new people, and hopefully ease the transition when it came time for Rosie to leave.

"It was my pleasure. Very thoughtful of you to try and help that young woman." Sage slipped her apron over her neck and then tied the straps around her slender waist. "I'm expecting a shipment of beans from Venezuela today. With any luck I'll have my first batch roasted today before I have to go home."

Very few chocolatiers made their chocolate from fermented and dried beans the way Sage did. In her place, Rosie wouldn't have bothered. But Sage was a purist and nothing made her happier than working through the complicated steps of roasting, cracking, grinding and conching the beans.

Artistic black and white photos, showing each step of the process, were framed on the wall behind the cash register. Of all the steps, Rosie was proficient only with the last one, that of tempering the chocolate so the fats achieved a chemical bond. The resulting product could then be used in any of their many chocolate products.

Working all day surrounded by the heady aromas of cocoa, vanilla, caramel, and a multitude of other delicious flavors never got old for her.

"When I move you have to send me care packages of chocolate."

Sage laughed. "I'm sure you'll find excellent chocolatiers in L.A."

"None as good as you." Rosie noticed the clock on the stove click over to ten. "Oops, I better go unlock the door."

The morning started with a rush on the hot chocolate, making Rosie glad she'd already prepared her first batch of the day in the heavy copper pan used solely for that purpose. The cooler autumn mornings seemed to be putting people in the mood for a warm and comforting beverage to start their day. The trend would only continue as they counted down the days to Halloween, then Thanksgiving and Christmas.

After the morning cocoa rush there was a quiet hour, then a steady pickup in business that kept Rosie on her feet all through lunch hour.

Though Rosie was glad to be busy, she couldn't help but

wish for a few lulls so she could work on her brother's script. What with the time she was spending with Sara Maria, working on the house with Brant—not to mention having a new roommate—she was finding it harder than ever to keep up with Daniel's output.

Last night, instead of helping Brant with the scraping, she should have kept fleshing out the scene Daniel needed. She'd only made it halfway through—no matter what, she had to finish it tonight after work.

But when she arrived home shortly after six and found Brant on a ladder, priming the window frames, she almost forgot her resolve. His long lean muscles were clearly visible under his basic white t-shirt and the smile of welcome he gave her was full of temptation.

"Want to join in the fun?"

"I'd love to. But I have a little project to work on tonight. Something for my brother."

He paused, obviously waiting for her to elaborate.

Rosie knew Daniel wouldn't mind at all if she told people she was working on the script with him. In fact he was keen for her to take her share of the profits and credit.

But up until now, she hadn't felt worthy, somehow. Daniel was the one with the ideas, he shaped the story and had the contacts and know-how to get a project accepted for production. She just filled in a few of the blanks with dialogue.

Lately though, she'd been doing a lot more. Soon she

would have to come clean about her involvement, especially if their screenplay actually went into production.

But not yet.

At the kitchen table Rosie found another note from Portia.

"Aunt Sage needs me to babysit tonight because Dawson is working and she's at a critical stage with her chocolate. I'll probably sleep over, so the house is yours!"

Rosie blushed at the implication.

But she also smiled, and continued to do so as she opened her laptop and picked up the scene where she'd left it last night.

Soon she was lost in the alternate universe of the small town drama devised by her brother. When Brant knocked at the screen door over an hour later, she was surprised to see it was dusk already.

"I've got to call it a day," Brant said. "I have an early morning tomorrow. Lots to do before I take my week off."

"Wait a minute. You're going on a holiday?" She saved her document and shut the laptop, before opening the screen door between them.

"Yeah, a relaxing holiday spent painting the house of this cute girl I just met."

Her face went hot and she couldn't help smiling. "Thanks for the compliment, but I don't want you using up your vacation doing this work for me."

"We're running out of time darlin'. According to the

weather network we've got a beautiful window of sunny, warm weather to get the job done now. Besides, I've got a bunch of banked vacation days."

Rosie didn't argue anymore, because she was running out of time as well. If her house was still on the market come November she might not be able to sell it until next spring. Maddie Cash had warned her it was difficult to sell a house during the holiday season.

"That's very sweet of you."

"Yeah. Isn't it?"

Oh, she loved that cocky smile of his. When he stepped forward to kiss her, she found herself melting even more.

"I wish I had more stew to offer. But we finished it last night."

"That's okay. I'm going to pick up a burger on my way out of town. See you tomorrow?"

One last kiss and he was gone.

FRIDAY MORNING WHEN Rosie awoke she found a text message from Portia confirming she'd stayed the night at Sage's and wouldn't be home until later that morning. She'd set up a lunch meeting with the owners of the Two Old Goats wine store—could Rosie meet her there at quarter past twelve?

"Yes, if Sage covers the shop for me."

A minute later Portia responded. *"Just asked her and she said sure."*

Rosie was putting on her mascara when she realized she hadn't seen Huck yet this morning. She put down the wand and went to look in her parents' bedroom. Sure enough Huck was fast asleep in his usual spot.

"Hey, Huck. Want to go out and then have some food?"

The old dog opened his eyes but didn't lift his head.

Her stomach tightened with concern. "Huck? Come on old boy. We can go for a walk if you want. How does that sound? Want to go for a walk?"

None of his favorite words—go out, food, walk—roused him.

This general pattern of apathy was really starting to worry her. She decided she would have to take him to the vet this morning if Dr. Sullivan could squeeze him in. A quick phone call confirmed he would.

"Okay, Huck, I'm going to have to insist you get up. Can you do it boy, or do I need to carry you?" Lifting him wouldn't be fun since Huck weighed an awkward forty-five pounds. So she was relieved when he finally, unsteadily, rose to his feet.

She didn't try to rush him as he slowly made his way to the back door. When he was finished his constitutional she filled his dish with his favorite food, laced with gravy. He sniffed but didn't partake.

"Okay. Into the car with you." Normally she walked him to the vet, it wasn't that far, but today that wasn't an option. With a boost he managed to scramble into the passenger side of her vehicle. A few minutes later, she was coaxing him into the front door of the clinic.

Despite a room full of waiting clients, Veronica, the older, white-haired receptionist was really sweet. She came out from behind her counter and gave Huck some TLC. "Not yourself today, are you, Huck?"

"He refused his breakfast. I had to struggle to get him to go outside to pee."

"Could be psychological. I'm sure he still misses your father. But we'll have to rule out medical causes, too. Dr. Sullivan is going to want to run a few tests. He suggested you leave Huck with us for a few hours, so we can squeeze the work in between our scheduled appointments. You okay with that?"

"I have to open the chocolate shop in ten minutes, so that would be awesome. You'll call me if there are any problems?"

"Absolutely." Veronica patted her arm. "And you, honey? How are you doing? I heard you aren't having much luck selling your family's old house."

"Not yet. But hopefully soon." Veronica was lovely, but she could be a bit too chatty. "I should get to work now." She crouched down to stroke her dog.

"Bye-bye, Huck. I'll be back soon, okay?"

The old lab gave her such a dejected look, she almost couldn't leave. But Veronica promised they'd take good care of him. So with one last pat, she finally left, saying a silent prayer that whatever was wrong, it wouldn't be serious.

THE TWO OLD Goats wine store was on Front Street beside the bridal store, Married in Marietta.

"For good reason." Clifford Yerks, one of the two sixty-plus-year-old men who owned the place, joked. "Anyone contemplating marriage is going to need to pair that insane decision with a well-aged and elegant cabernet sauvignon."

Rosie looked at Portia. Both laughed.

"Let me just say," Emerson Moore said, "we're really excited about this idea of yours. We frequently do wine tastings, but partnering with Sage's chocolate shop really has us inspired."

"I'm so glad to hear that." Portia placed a large copper-colored box on the center of the round table at the back of the store where all four were seated. "Sage included samples here of ten of our most popular chocolates. From these she was hoping you could choose five that would make good wine-pairing menu items for our event.

"Oh, yummy. We get to sample?" Clifford rubbed his hands together.

Of the two men—who'd moved to Marietta five years ago after retiring from jobs on Wall Street—Clifford appeared to be the one with the biggest sweet tooth, since his girth was about double his partner's.

"Absolutely," Portia said. "We've brought along two of

each type of chocolate."

"That would mean ten chocolates each!" Emerson protested. "We're going to need a knife."

"Are we?" Clifford checked his partner's expression then added in a resigned tone, "Yes, I guess we are."

Once the knife had been procured, Rosie donned a pair of latex gloves then expertly sliced each sample chocolate into halves. One by one the men took their tastes, jotting down notes on each chocolate before cleansing their palates with small squares of French bread and sips of water.

Just watching them taste the chocolates was comical. Rosie had seen lots of happy customers savor Sage's chocolates. But these men seemed to become one with the chocolate.

"Did you get that hint of tobacco in the single origin?" Emerson asked.

"Yes. I'm thinking merlot, something with concentrated fruit notes."

On and on the discussion went, and they hadn't moved past the first five samples. Rosie realized that the hour she'd agreed upon with Sage wasn't going to be nearly enough time.

A glance at Portia confirmed she was thinking the same thing.

"How about we leave these with you," Rosie suggested. "And you get back to us with your ideas on which would be most suitable?"

The men were so focused on their task they didn't seem

to hear at first. Finally Clifford took note and rose from his chair.

"Thank you so much, lovely ladies. We are going to come up with a kick-ass menu for your event."

"Elegantly put," Emerson said drily. "But I'm sure they get the gist. We will call you soon."

"Wonderful," Rosie said. But the men had already turned their attention back to the chocolate.

ROSIE WONDERED IF Brant would show up at five-thirty as usual that Friday afternoon. She was alone in the shop, Sage having left hours ago along with Portia who wanted to use her aunt's color printer to make a poster for their event.

Rosie told herself it didn't really matter, since she'd be seeing Brant every day for the next week as painted her house.

Still, her heart jumped happily when she saw him stride by the display window, pausing as usual by the chocolate shop door.

Also as per usual, he removed his hat after he entered the store. The smile he gave her this time, though, was a lot more personal.

"Good afternoon, cowboy. May I offer you a sample of our chocolate mint melt away today?"

His smile broadened. "No ma'am, you may not. I'm here for my regular."

"And nothing I can offer will tempt you…"

He lowered his voice and it came out sounding rich and husky. "We've already determined you can tempt me. Just not by anything currently for sale in that chocolate counter of yours."

"Is that so, sir," she said demurely. She pulled a box from under the counter, already wrapped and ready to go. "Your dozen salted chocolate caramels, as per usual."

Before he could pull out his wallet, she shook her head. "This one is on me, cowboy."

"There's no need for you to do that."

"Yes there is when you've been spending every spare hour you've got painting my house."

"I'd still feel better—"

"I insist, cowboy. This one is on the house. So to speak."

They both chuckled, and Brant leaned an arm on the divider between them. "How about you join my sister and me for our pizza and movie tonight?"

She hesitated. Friday night was the one bit of dedicated time Brant reserved for Sara Maria. She wasn't sure she should bust into it.

"Trust me, you'll make Sara Maria just as happy as me if you say yes."

Sadly, she believed that was true. So she agreed.

"Awesome." He took the bag with the chocolates. "You're closing at six, right? Want me to help?"

"No, I've already taken care of everything. I just need to

lock up and go. Why don't you take the chocolates to Sara Maria. I'll meet you both at the pizza parlor. I need to take Huck home from the vet first."

Brant frowned. "He sick?"

"Wouldn't eat anything this morning and was so lethargic I could hardly coax him to go out and do his business, so I dropped him off for a checkup this morning. Dr. Sullivan called me a few hours ago. The good news is that physically he's fine. The bad news is the vet believes Huck is suffering from a prolonged depression after the death of my father. And there's not much I can do about that."

"Poor fella. I hope he perks up soon." Brant slapped his hat back on his head. "See you in about thirty minutes?"

"Perfect." Once he was gone she hustled to the kitchen and whipped off her apron. Not only did she want to make sure Huck was okay, but she also planned to change into one of the outfits she and Portia had ordered online.

Chapter Thirteen

"WHAT DO YOU say if Rosie joins us for pizza and a movie tonight?" Brant knew he was pushing his luck, talking to Sara Maria while she was watching her program.

Without taking her attention off the screen, though, Sara Maria calmly said, "That's good."

He'd already given her the chocolates and now he was just waiting until the credits rolled on the game show so they could get moving.

"What is China," Sara Maria said.

And, yes, she was correct.

A growing sense of pride warmed his chest as he watched his sister nail the world history category. Recalling Rosie's comment about Sara Maria's reading choices, he glanced around the room until he spotted the book of writings from Immanuel Kant, bookmarked well beyond the half-way point.

Why was his sister so smart in some ways—so extraordinarily smart—yet stunted in others? Undone by change in routine, curtailed by disabling anxiety, forgetful, and careless regarding certain rules of basic safety…

When she'd had that breakdown after their mother's death, he'd thought that was it for her. That she'd be unable to function at the level she'd been maintaining up until then.

He had to admit she'd proved him wrong. She was almost back to her normal now and, in some ways, actually growing stronger, as if, without Mom around to cushion her, she was learning new coping strategies.

There was no doubt this home was no longer the right place for her. But where was? Even her doctors admitted she wasn't a good candidate for independent living.

Finally the show was over, including the credits. Sara Maria powered off the television.

"Let's go."

He jumped to his feet. As usual they were quiet during their walk to the pizza parlor. They were placing their drink orders when Rosie made her entrance.

And it was some entrance.

His request for three colas and glasses of water died in his throat. Rosie looked incredible. She'd changed into a flowing skirt and silky blouse and was wearing heels that made her legs look even longer and slimmer than usual.

Best of all, she wore her hair loose and curly, the way he liked it.

Getting to his feet, he waited until she was seated next to Sara Maria before he settled back down.

"Looking pretty fine, Miss Rosie."

"I'm glad you think so. Sorry I'm late. It was hard to leave Huck, even though I know I'm not the person he wants to be with."

"Who does he want to be with?" Sara Maria asked.

"My dad. The vet says he misses him a lot and that's why he's so depressed."

"We shouldn't leave him alone." Sara Maria dropped her menu. "We can order our pizza to go and watch a movie on your television. That way Huck will have lots of company."

"Hang on," Brant said. "Who says Rosie wants us tramping over to her place?"

"But I do. I think it's an excellent suggestion." It was also pretty amazing that the suggestion had come from Sara Maria. Apparently she wasn't as wedded to her routines as Brant had thought.

THIRTY MINUTES LATER, they were all settled in Rosie's living room with their cans of sodas and an extra-large vegetarian pizza open on the coffee table. Brant sat on the sofa cushion next to Rosie, letting his hand graze the back of her neck, creating shivers of pleasure she tried hard to hide. At first Rosie worried Sara Maria would notice and comment, but she was totally focused on Huck, calling and calling for him to join them.

Finally Huck made his appearance, his nails clacking on

the hardwood as he ambled from his rug in Rosie's parents' room. When he settled on the floor at Sara Maria's feet, Sara Maria slid down beside him. Huck promptly laid his head on her lap, and she rested one hand on his back while eating pizza with the other.

A less polite dog might have taken advantage of the situation, but Huck showed no interest in sneaking a bite of pizza.

Given his poor appetite lately, if he had, Rosie would have happily looked the other way.

But he seemed content just to be near Sara Maria. Nothing more, nothing less.

Picking a movie proved complicated. Sara Maria had seen everything she considered worthwhile that was available on Netflix. When Rosie brought out her parents' old DVD collection, however, Sara Maria pounced on *Jerry Maguire.*

"I've always wanted to see that. It's been highly rated by some of the better critics."

Rosie did a double take. Sometimes Sara Maria sounded like a college professor when she spoke.

"I'd like to see it as well," Brant said. "You, Rosie?"

"It's one of my favorites. I never get tired of it." Though it was definitely the sort of movie she'd have preferred watching just the two of them. Especially the scene where Jerry kisses Dorothy good night for the first time... On second thought it was probably too soon in their relationship to watch a scene like that alone.

Or was it?

Rosie felt a flush of excitement as she imagined what it would be like to be kissed by Brant so intensely. Was it wicked to hope Brant might pick up a few ideas from this movie?

Well, even it was, she didn't care. Maybe she and Brant didn't have a future, but they had chemistry, no doubt about that.

And right now, it seemed like more than enough.

As Rosie slotted the DVD into the player, Portia came in via the kitchen entrance. She took the presence of their visitors totally in stride.

"Hey there, Brant. And you must be Sara Maria. Nice to meet you."

"Did you finish the posters?" Rosie asked.

"Sure did. I stopped to put one up at our store on my way home. Make sure you admire it tomorrow." Portia turned to the TV screen where the movie was just starting. "Hey you're watching *Jerry Maguire.* My sister thinks that's Tom Cruise's best movie."

"I agree. Sit down and watch it with us." Rosie settled back into her spot next to Brant, secretly thrilled when he stretched his arm along the back of the sofa and stroked her neck again.

"There's lots of pizza and cola," Brant added.

"Cool." Portia grabbed a slice of the pizza then settled in one of the armchairs. She smiled at the girl and dog curled up beside her. "Hey, Sara Maria, looks like Huck is totally in love with you."

"I'm totally in love with him, too." Sara Maria pressed her cheek against the top of the lab's head.

"Well, Rosie does need to find a new home for him when she moves," Portia said, probably thinking she was being helpful.

"Rosie's moving?" Sara Maria looked alarmed.

"Once my house sells, I will be." She held her breath, wondering if this would spark a tantrum, but though she looked sad, Sara Maria didn't display any inappropriate reaction.

"You aren't taking Huck?"

"I'll be moving to L.A. Huck wouldn't be happy in a big city."

"No pets are allowed at the care home because of allergies," Sara Maria said. "But I wish I could keep Huck. He completes me."

Rosie gave the younger woman a close look. "I thought you said you hadn't seen this movie?"

To her utter amazement, Sara Maria winked back at her.

THE NEXT FEW days were crazy busy. On Saturday, Rosie worked a full shift at the chocolate shop while Brant finished priming all the window frames and doors. He left for Three Bars Ranch, exhausted, at seven-thirty, at which point Rosie picked up her laptop and resumed writing the next scene for her brother's script.

The flow felt awkward, though, and she couldn't pinpoint why. Rosie decided to print out the troublesome pages. Sometimes she could spot problems easier on paper than on her laptop.

As the printer in her parents' bedroom spewed out the sheets, she decided to try working at her dad's desk, see if some of his creative powers might wear off on her.

It felt strange at first, sitting in his chair, at his desk. But she knew if he were watching he'd be glad to see her here. Her father had always encouraged her writing, just as much as he'd encouraged Daniel's.

On Sunday, Rosie dragged herself out of bed after a scant six hours of sleep and went to pick up Sara Maria for the day. As they were exiting the care home, Rosie recognized one of the nurses from when she had worked for Rosie's mom's GP. "Hi, Annie, how are you?"

"Rosie! It's so good to see you. I heard you were coming around regularly to take our youngest resident on outings." The petite woman with her wavy hair and lively brown eyes smiled at Sara Maria.

"Rosie's my new friend.

"That's real nice to hear." She turned to Rosie. "I was talking to Nadine the other day about how Sara Maria has perked up recently. It's good for her to socialize with people her own age. What are you all up to today?"

"I'm not sure." Rosie had been taken aback by her first sight of Sara Maria this morning. Brant's sister was far from a fashionista, but she'd hit a new low today with her ragged jeans and a t-shirt with an obvious bleach stain at the hem. "Maybe we'll go hiking?"

Sara Maria surprised her by shaking her head no. "I want to help paint your house."

Rosie planted her hands on her hips and swiveled for a closer look at her. "Seriously?"

"I think it will be fun."

"I can't afford to pay much."

"I don't want to be paid. I'll paint for free."

Annie laughed. "Do you think you could give my fence a fresh coat while you're in the mood?"

Sara Maria didn't get the joke. "No. I just want to paint Rosie's house. I like her house and I especially like her dog, Huck."

"Okay then. I guess we're spending the day painting." Though Rosie had serious doubts about whether Sara Maria would enjoy painting as much as she seemed to think she would.

When they arrived at the house, Brant was just stepping out of his truck.

"I'm going to help you paint Rosie's house," his sister announced.

"Is that so?" He looked from Rosie to his sister, then back again. From his raised eyebrows, Rosie guessed he was dubious about Sara Maria's painting abilities, too.

"Sure you wouldn't rather go hiking with Rosie?"

For her answer, Sara Maria picked up a paint brush.

"Okay then." He gave a resigned sigh. "Here's how it works."

Brant demonstrate the basic technique and after watching him for a minute, Sara Maria dipped her brush and mimicked him.

"Not bad." Brant watched her a while longer.

While Sara Maria painted slowly, she was also meticulous, so Brant assigned her a couple of window frames. Meanwhile he and Rosie traded their paint brushes for rollers. "These are great for applying paint quickly, but there will be splatters. Best wear something to protect that crazy hair of yours."

"I put my hair in a very tidy ponytail today, so I object to the adjective 'crazy'."

From his truck Brant retrieved an L.A. Dodgers baseball cap. "Object to my adjectives all you want, you still need to wear a cap. And since you're moving to L.A. you'll have to start cheering for these guys."

She started backing away. "No way. I'd feel like a traitor to the Mariners."

He pulled her closer, then planted the hat on her head. "They're in different leagues."

"It's still baseball." She twisted away, then removed her hat and flung it at him.

He caught it easily and promptly placed it back on her head.

"Jeez. Sara Maria is your brother always this bossy?"

Sara Maria's "Yes!" was so heartfelt Rosie had to laugh. Brant didn't look amused though.

They painted all day long with only short breaks for lemonade and muffins. When it was time for Sara Maria to return to the home for dinner, Rosie asked if she would rather eat with them, but apparently Sunday's dinner at the care home was always vegetarian lasagna—one of Sara Maria's favorites.

"Okay." Rosie conceded. "I'll drive you home on my way to pick up take-out burgers for your brother and myself."

Sara Maria grimaced at the mention of burgers, and happily washed the last of the paint from her hands.

On the short drive to the care home Rosie said, "Thanks for all your hard work today. You remember that you're meeting Rachel from the Gingerbread and Dessert Shop tomorrow right?"

"I remember."

"The care home has organized a ride for you. Have you decided what to wear?"

"No. What should I wear, Rosie? Does it matter?"

"This is basically a job interview, so, yes, it does matter. Do you have black pants and a white shirt?"

"Yes."

"Good. Wear that. And you'll probably be invited into

Rachel's kitchen, so tie your hair in a ponytail."

"Okay."

Rosie stopped in front of the care home. "Good luck tomorrow."

Sara Maria swallowed. In a quiet voice she asked, "What if Rachel doesn't like me?"

"Just keep reminding yourself that you make really good pies. That's what Rachel is interested in. If you believe in yourself, then Rachel will believe in you, too."

"That isn't very logical. But I can see how that might work. Thanks, Rosie."

"See you soon. And thanks again for today. You did an awesome job with the window frames."

Rosie waited until Sara Maria was safely inside, then she headed for the Main Street Diner to get burgers, fries, and milkshakes to go. After all their hard work they'd earned the treat.

She and Brant ate on the porch swing at the front of the house, Rosie turning on the strands of outdoor patio lights as the sun sank lower.

Huck, who'd followed Sara Maria around all day, was sleeping on the far edge of the porch now. Brant tried tossing him a French fry. The lab didn't even give it a sniff.

"I'm worried about the old boy."

"Was he always your dad's dog?"

"From day one. When Huck was a puppy I was still going to school, Mom was working full time, and Daniel was already in L.A. So he spent his days with Dad, sleeping by his desk while Dad wrote. Dad would take him out for a walk in the morning after breakfast and again at the end of the day when he'd finished his pages."

"Well, no wonder Huck's depressed. His entire world has changed." After a paused Brant added, "A lot like my sister's has."

Rosie was glad to see Brant display some empathy for his sister. "She seemed pretty happy helping us paint today."

"It was a good day." Brant put his arm around her shoulders.

"Speak for yourself. My neck and arms are aching."

Despite her cheeky words, her heart felt giddy, like a stone, skipping over water. She had the same reaction every time he touched her, heck, all he had to do was look at her. There was a certain gleam in his eyes, a knowing quirk in his grin.

"Poor baby." He brushed his hand across her back to her neck, then began working his fingers into her muscles. "How does that feel?"

"Lovely."

He continued the massage for about five minutes, then he shifted slightly, so he could look at her face. They were screened from the street by a hedge of lilacs, leaves all gold, but still clinging to their branches. So even though they were in the middle of a small town, it felt like they were entirely alone.

"Too tired for me to kiss you?" Brant asked.

"Don't think I could ever be *that* tired."

"Ah, Rosie. I feel the same way."

He kissed her on the lips first, then on the cheek and her jawline. Gently, he nuzzled the side of her neck, the ridge of her collarbone.

Her nerve endings danced at each point he touched. Rosie closed her eyes, savored the sweet sensations, until finally he drew her close into a hug.

"Ah, Rosie. You make it so difficult for me to be a gentleman."

She wanted to ask him what was so great about being a gentleman. But a vehicle had just stopped in front of their house. She had a feeling it was Portia, and Brant seemed to take it as a hint to leave.

"You don't have to go."

"I should. I've got a lot of work to get done tomorrow."

"I'll be helping, too."

"I thought you worked at the chocolate shop on Mondays?"

"Dakota and I switched shifts again. You said we're running out of time this late in the season. I felt I had to do my part, as well."

"Thank you for that." He kissed her one last time, then got up from the porch swing. "Sleep well, darlin'."

"You, too," Rosie said softly.

He went around the house to where he'd parked his

truck in the lane. Meanwhile Rosie heard the faint squeak of the front gate as Portia returned.

She seemed surprised to see Rosie sitting outside on the porch.

"Hey, there. Aren't you a little cool?"

Now that Brant was no longer by her side, she was.

"You're right. Time to go inside." Rosie grabbed the paper bag from their takeout dinner, and then nudged Huck toward the door.

Once they were all inside she asked Portia, "So how was your day?"

"I spent most of it on the Circle C. Aunt Callan owns some really sweet quarter horses. I especially like a beautiful grey gelding named Pinstripes."

"Cute name for a horse." Rosie followed Portia through the family room to the kitchen. "So what were you doing on the ranch?"

"Aunt Callan and I went on an awesome trail ride. My mom and Aunt Sage are both amazing riders, but Callan is something else. I'd love for you to meet her."

"I've seen her in the shop a few times. She's always in a hurry."

"She's so tough on the outside but a real softie where it counts. Usually when we're around one another it's a big family occasion. It's been fun getting to know her better."

"You're lucky to have such a large family. My parents were both single children and I can barely remember my grandparents, they passed away so long ago."

"Yeah, it is good to have lots of aunts. But I wish I saw more of my dad." Portia stooped to give Huck a cuddle. "He hasn't been around much since he left my mom."

"I'm sorry." Though her parents had been plagued by bad health in their final years, she'd always felt lucky that, for the time they'd had together, they'd been very happy.

"Yeah. It sucks." Portia stood and then shrugged one of her slim shoulders. "What about you? Did you spend your entire weekend painting?"

"When I wasn't working, yes." Daniel would be upset that she still hadn't finished that last scene. Rosie resolved to stay up as late as it took tonight to do it.

"I hope you don't mind that I haven't been helping. But being pregnant…"

Rosie suddenly felt like an idiot. "Duh. Right. Being around paint fumes probably isn't a smart idea for you right now. Oh, my gosh. I'm so sorry, Portia. I should have realized…"

"No, no don't worry. What else could you have done? You need to sell your house and this is going to help so much."

"Do you think the odor inside the house is too much?"

"I'm not sure. But I'd rather not take a risk. Especially since there's loads of room at the Circle C ranch and it's not that far from Marietta. Callan said she'd love to have me stay there for a while—and I can help her exercise some of her horses in my spare time."

"That does sound ideal. But I've really enjoyed having you as a roommate."

"It's been great for me, too. But now that Brant is in the picture... I'm a bit of third wheel."

"No. I wasn't thinking that at all."

"I'm just teasing. But I do think my moving out to the Circle C is the right solution. My parents bred and trained Tennessee Walkers when I was growing up. I used to ride almost every day and I miss it."

"Since I haven't cashed your check yet, I'll just rip it up. But—I'm going to miss you."

"Me, too. We'll see each other at the chocolate shop, though. And we can go for lunch. You're my best friend in this town, Rosie."

"I feel the same way."

Why were all the nicest people coming into her life now as she was preparing to leave?

Chapter Fourteen

O N MONDAY, ROSIE didn't feel ready to get out of bed at eight o'clock. She'd been awake until after two a.m. when she'd finally emailed the closing scene to Daniel. Hopefully he agreed she'd nailed the dialogue between the two main characters and found just the right narrative twist to end the script with a bittersweet sense of inevitability.

By eight thirty, she couldn't make any more excuses. She dragged herself into the shower, and then let Huck out into the yard. Was he a little livelier this morning, or was that just her wishful thinking?

Brant showed up at nine sharp. From the kitchen window, Rosie enjoyed watching him step out of his truck in his form-fitting Wranglers, paint splotched from yesterday, and a clean white t-shirt.

She slipped out the screen door, letting it fall shut behind her.

"Coffee?" She proffered a mug.

He stepped toward her with a warm, lazy smile. "Wish every work day could start this sweet." He lingered with one soft kiss before accepting the mug.

"It's supposed to be a hot one today," he said after his first sip. "I was thinking we'd start on the west side, then tackle the north around noon."

"Sounds like a plan," she agreed.

Rosie brought out her iPod docking system and plugged it into an exterior socket so she could play some of her country favorites. They worked hard all morning through to the afternoon, eventually turning down the music because it was making it hard to chat. Several times Brant made her laugh so hard with his stories from working on the ranch she had to stop painting and wait to catch her breath.

At two-thirty Rosie's cell phone rang. She whipped it out of her back pocket and checked the display. No name. She rattled off the number and was surprised when Brant said, "That's my sister."

"I didn't know Sara Maria had a cell phone."

"I'd forgotten myself." Brant shrugged. "This is the first time I've known her to use it."

Rosie pressed "Accept."

"Hey, Sara Maria. How are you?"

"I'm so happy. Rosie, I got a job! Rachel had me roll out a pie crust and as soon as I was done, she asked if I could start tomorrow. She wants me to work in her kitchen on Tuesdays and Fridays. On Tuesday I bake pies and on Friday I help with cleaning and organizing ingredients for other recipes."

"Fantastic! Good for you."

"This means I won't be able to help you paint tomorrow, though."

"Don't worry about that. I think it's great that you have a job."

"Me, too. Bye, Rosie."

The line went quiet before Rosie could reply. Cleary when Sara Maria decided a conversation was over, it was over. Rosie tucked her phone into her pocket. "Did you hear that? Your sister's been hired to work two days a week at a local bakery."

"Is that so?" Brant looked skeptical. "I hope whoever did the hiring knows what they're getting into."

"The day she baked those pies she also rearranged my cabinets. I was skeptical but I have to admit it's a lot more functional now. Your sister knows her way around a kitchen. I'm sure she'll be fine."

"All the same, I better pay a visit to this bakery. Make sure they know Sara Maria needs to be supervised."

"Are you sure that she does?"

"I told you about all the smoke alarms she set off, right?" Brant opened a fresh can of paint, then climbed back up the ladder.

"Well, I've done dumb things, too. Left a candle burning once all night long. I was lucky it was sitting on a glass table and not wood."

"This is different, Rosie. Trust me."

They returned to their painting. After he finished his current section, Brant moved around the corner. It seemed hardly any time had passed when Rosie noticed how long the shadows were getting. By seven Brant suggested it was getting too dark to do a proper job. They cleaned up and then crashed with exhaustion on the front porch.

"I feel guilty about you working so hard on my house when you could be doing things with your sister."

"Rosie, please, let's not go through this again. Sara Maria and I have our routine. Our Friday night dinners and movies work well for both of us."

Rosie saw no point in arguing, even though she disagreed. She remembered her mom telling her once that some people were just no good with babies. They were so afraid of doing the wrong thing, they couldn't just relax and enjoy.

It seemed Brant was like that with his sister. And maybe he always would be. It was a depressing thought.

"Come on, darlin', we've been working real hard. How about we go to Grey's Saloon and kick back for a few hours—have some beer and do some dancing?"

Despite her exhaustion, Rosie was tempted. She'd checked her messages earlier and Daniel was thrilled with the new ending. That meant she could take the entire night off for a change.

"Hm. I guess that means I need to take a shower."

"I could help with that." He stood, then held out his hands to her.

"You *could*. But you *won't*." After Rosie allowed him to pull her up, she pointed him in the direction of her parents' bedroom. "Fresh towels are in the en suite."

"And where are you going?"

"My bathroom is down the hall, cowboy. And you are not invited." Rosie smiled before turning her back on him.

Brant gave out a mock groan of disappointment.

Once in the shower, however, Rosie couldn't help wondering. How much longer would she have the willpower to hold Brant at arm's length?

Even though she thought he was misguided about his sister, every time she saw him she was falling a little deeper. Then there was her upcoming move to L.A.—assuming her house sold. There were so many reasons for her to be putting the brakes on this new relationship.

Yet here she was, going out with the guy for a night of drinking and dancing.

And she couldn't remember the last time she'd felt so happy.

MONDAY NIGHT FOOTBALL was playing when Rosie entered Grey's Saloon on Brant's arm. She felt pretty tonight, partly because she was wearing another of the outfits she'd ordered with Portia online—a floral dress with a cute, denim jacket, paired with her favorite cowboy boots—and partly because of the way Brant kept looking at her.

Before they even sat down Rosie saw someone she knew. "See that woman laughing over there? That's my real estate agent."

As soon as Brant turned to look, Maddie spotted them and waved them over.

After Rosie made introductions, Maddie said, "I drove by your place this morning and noticed you're in the process of repainting. Smart move."

"I should have listened to you sooner," Rosie admitted.

"Better late than never. I'd like to meet with you later this week. Discuss some strategies to drum up some buyers. Would lunch on Wednesday work?"

"Sure."

"Maybe you could bring a little something from the chocolate shop for dessert?"

Maddie winked and Rosie laughed. Maddie was a self-professed chocoholic and one of their best customers. "That goes without saying, Maddie."

After a bit more chat, Brant led Rosie to the bar where they ordered beer and chicken wings. A group of off duty firefighters was at the table behind them, having fun but making a bit too much noise. Brant suggested they move into one of the corner tables. The farthest one was already occupied by a man with a languid posture, nursing a beer.

"Looks like he's had a rough day." Brant commented as they moved to the other corner.

"That's Trey Reyes. He's an investigator. I wonder if he's

working a case?" She glanced around the room trying to guess who could be the subject of Trey's scrutiny.

"Maybe he's just a guy who wants a beer?" Brant touched the tip of her nose. "Let me guess. You liked to read Nancy Drew when you were a child."

"Not in particular but I did love mysteries. I wanted to be Harriet the spy so badly. For about a year I pretended I was."

"That must have been cute." Brant pushed the plate of chicken wings toward her. "You need to eat, girl. You worked hard today."

Yes, she had worked hard, but sitting here with Brant, so close their thighs were touching, made food the last thing she cared about. Fortunately, the game finally went into halftime and someone lowered the volume and started up a Zac Brown song on the juke box. She didn't even have to hint. Brant was already standing, holding out his hand.

"Would the lady like to dance?"

"Hell, yes."

She could tell within ten seconds that Brant was a natural on the dance floor. He had moves with his two-step she'd never seen before, but Brant was so adept at leading she floated and swayed right along with him.

The next song was slower, and Brant pulled her in nice and tight, resting the side of his face against the top of her head. She felt like they were riding a wave on the ocean, both of them clinging together, generating a pulsing, electric heat that wiped every rational thought out of her head.

When the firefighters called out that the game had started and could someone please turn up the volume, Brant suggested they leave. He left money on the table, then put his arm around her shoulders, holding her like she was something precious to him.

The night air was fresh and the autumn leaves crunched under their feet as they walked the five blocks back to Rosie's house. A lot of houses were decorated for Halloween already with pumpkins and lights and witches and ghosts. Rosie directed Brant to the longer route along Bramble Lane, where the larger estate homes were especially well decorated.

All except one house, however, dark and neglected among the other fine homes, and almost hidden from view by ancient pine trees.

"What's with this place?" Brant asked.

"Judge Kingsley lives here. He's a bit of a curmudgeon though, to be fair, Mom said he was a pretty decent guy before his grandson died in some sort of awful tragedy. I'm not sure of the details."

A gust of wind caused the branch of one of the trees to make a peculiar moaning sound and Rosie started.

Brant's arm tightened around her. "Don't be scared, Rosie. I'll protect you from the evil spirits."

Yes, but who will protect me from you?

Not that she wanted protecting. She'd already decided this would be the night. She was crazy about this cowboy.

She'd been the good daughter for long enough. This was her chance to live. To enjoy life to the fullest.

On the front porch, he pulled her close again and kissed her.

This kiss was different from the others. Needier. Harder. It turned her limbs to jelly and set her heart on fire.

"I've probably had too much beer tonight to drive back to Bozeman," he whispered next to her ear. "You know anyone who might put me up for the night?"

She put her arms around his waist and gazed up at him. "You didn't need to play that card, cowboy. You had me at hello."

WHEN IT CAME to making love, living for the moment meant appreciating every inch of a beautiful woman. What Brant realized that night, as he took Rosie to her bed, was that she might well be the most beautiful woman he'd ever known. The key to her appeal was in her eyes and he found himself staring into them a lot that evening.

He needed to know what she liked, how she felt, what she needed. Her eyes told him all of that.

And a lot more.

"Don't be shy. Don't hold back. Not with me, Rosie."

She trusted him.

He made love to her not only as if it were the first time, which it was, but like it was the last time as well, which he certainly hoped it wasn't. Still, their time together would be limited and he wanted each moment to count. To be real and special.

Later, when he'd given her every pleasure it was in his power to give, he held her in his arms and watched her fall asleep.

Though he wasn't usually given to the sort of ruminating that kept a man awake at night, Brant didn't drop off nearly as quickly. Insomnia wasn't so bad, though, when he had Rosie to feel and watch.

Every now and then his thoughts strayed to next week, to the snows of November, and the Christmas holidays.

Where would Rosie be by then?

No. Don't think that way.

And finally he slept.

"ROSIE, I'M NOT in any position to give out romantic advice. But what's going on with you and Brant?" Portia asked.

Rosie continued to measure coffee grounds into the machine. It wasn't yet eight but Portia had forgotten to pack her makeup kit and since she still had a key, she'd let herself in. She'd walked in apologizing, but her words had died out as her gaze travelled from Rosie's tousled hair, to the white oversized t-shirt she was wearing—which happened to be Brant's—and finally to Brant's truck parked in the back.

Brant was still sleeping and all Rosie wanted was to put

on some coffee then crawl back into bed with him. She'd been with a few men before but what she'd experienced with Brant last night had led her to understand what women meant when they said a man had "rocked my world."

Her world had been rocked all right.

And she wanted it to happen again.

"It looks like things are getting pretty serious. Will this affect your decision to move to L.A.?"

"My plans haven't changed," Rosie said calmly, closing the lid on the machine and pressing the start button. "I'm living in the moment. Having some fun for a change."

Portia leaned her back to the counter and crossed her arms over her chest. "That's fine for some people. But I'm not sure it's your style."

"It hasn't been. But I'm tired of being dull Rosie, the dutiful daughter. While I was giving my father twice-daily insulin injections, driving him to his specialist appointments in Bozeman, and preparing all his meals, other kids my age were out having fun, dancing, drinking, romancing. I'm long overdue in the fun department."

"I hear you. But I've done all those things you wish you'd done. Flirting with guys, drinking too much, dancing all night... In the long run none of that made me happy."

Portia stroked her belly pointedly. "You've got to be careful Rosie."

"We used protection, if that's what you mean."

"Glad to hear it. But it's not as easy to protect the heart.

Believe me, I know."

That gave Rosie pause. She studied her friend more closely, noticing the shadows under her eyes, the frailness of her shoulders. In just the short while she'd known Portia, she was pretty sure she'd lost a few pounds.

"How was your first night at the Circle C? Did you sleep well?"

Portia shrugged. "I slept some."

"And have you eaten yet this morning?"

"Way to turn the tables. I thought I was the one giving the lecture here."

"You care about me, and I appreciate that. But I'm worried about your lack of appetite and the effect on the baby."

"I was, too. But Doctor Bennion says it's not uncommon for a woman to lose a bit of weight in her first trimester as the body adjusts to the onslaught of all those hormones."

"Okay. Good to know."

The two friends smiled at each other.

"Now, I'm sorry I killed your good mood. I'll just grab my makeup and be out of here in a sec." She was halfway down the hall when she remembered something. "Could you drop by the chocolate shop this afternoon? The men from the Two Old Goats wine store have sent us their list of pairings and I'd love to show you."

"Will do." As Rosie waited for the coffee, she heard Portia enter the guest room that had been hers, then leave through the front door.

Shortly after that running water sounded from her bathroom, signaling Brant was up. The moment to join him in bed was lost. But they could still have breakfast together.

Rosie took two mugs from the cabinet, her mood not quite as cheerful as before. In her heart of hearts, she knew there was some truth in what Portia had said. She was taking a calculated risk by getting so involved with Brant. But it was too late now to change what had happened. And no matter how it ended, Rosie couldn't imagine ever regretting last night.

As she popped in bread for toast, Brant came up behind her and his arms encircled her waist.

"Good morning, gorgeous. Were you talking to yourself?"

She turned around so she could see his face. The shadow from his two-day beard only made him look more attractive.

"That was Portia. She dropped in for some stuff she'd left behind yesterday."

"No doubt she saw I'd spent the night. Did she approve?"

"Not really. But she's gone through some rough times lately with her own love life. She was just trying to protect me."

"Aren't you happy with what happened last night?" He slid his hands up her arms to her shoulders and looked deeply into her eyes.

"Very. And you—"

"Would have been happier if you were still in bed when I

woke up. But you made coffee, so I forgive you." He kissed her on the nose, then went to the coffee machine and filled their mugs.

"Peanut butter or jam on your toast? Or would you prefer some eggs?"

"Whatever you're having will be fine."

"Peanut butter it is."

They took their coffees and toast to the backyard, so they could admire their handiwork while they ate breakfast.

"It's really looking great, isn't it?"

"Yup. With you helping the job is going faster than I expected. I'll put the first coat of aqua on the front door today. I bet we have the entire house finished by Friday."

Within twenty minutes they were painting again. As she worked, Rosie wondered how Sara Maria's first day at the bakery was going. She could tell Brant was thinking the same thing when he said, "At noon I'm going to drop by that gingerbread bakery place. Can you tell me where it is?"

"You going to check on Sara Maria?"

"And talk to her boss. Make sure she knows what she's getting into."

"I'll only tell you where the bakery is if you promise to be tactful."

"Aren't I always?"

Rosie groaned. "It's on Main, just down from Grey's Saloon. But please, Brant, try to not embarrass your sister. This job is important to her."

Chapter Fifteen

ROSIE DECIDED TO walk downtown with Brant. While he checked in at the bakery, she could stop in at the chocolate shop and review the wine pairings list with Portia. She made Brant wait while she washed and changed into clean jeans and a turquoise tunic with pretty embroidery at the neck and along the sleeves. This was the last of her new purchases and she had to admit Portia had steered her right in all her choices.

"I'll grab us something to eat at the bakery," Brant promised, when it came time to separate.

"Great. And I'll buy us some lattes at the Java Cafe." Rosie knew she'd need a caffeine pick-me-up if she hoped to be productive this afternoon.

"Black coffee for me," Brant reminded her.

He gave her a smile and a kiss, then went on his way. Rosie hesitated outside the entrance. A poster advertising the Dark Magic Chocolate and Wine Tasting event, from seven to nine on the night of October thirty-first had been affixed to the front window display. Portia had done a great job with it. The colors, the fonts, the layout, all looked professional.

"Buy your tickets inside," the poster said.

Impulsively Rosie decided to purchase two tickets for herself and Brant. Was it tempting fate to gamble that they would still be seeing one another more than two weeks from now?

She hoped not.

Inside she found Portia chatting with two women who each carried a paper bag with the Copper Mountain Chocolates logo. It seemed Portia was also trying to convince the women to sign up for the tasting.

"That sounds lovely," one of the women said. "But I need to check with my husband."

"Me, too," said her friend, who might possibly have been her sister.

With their pageboy hair styles and medium-sized frames, the women looked remarkably similar.

"If the men don't want to go, you could always have a girls' night out," Portia said brightly.

"That might be fun! Olivia, what do you say? Should we do it?"

"Why not?"

While Portia took care of the paperwork, Rosie slipped into the kitchen area. Sage was filling pumpkin-shaped molds with creamy milk chocolate, a delicate operation Rosie knew better than to interrupt.

"Hi, Sage, how are you doing?"

When Sage barely grunted in return, Rosie decided it would be prudent to leave. Back in the store Portia was seeing the customers out the door. Once they were gone she heaved a sigh, then rubbed her hands together.

"Our first two registrants! Isn't this wonderful?"

"I want to buy two tickets as well," Rosie said.

"For you and Brant?"

Rosie hesitated, then nodded.

"Good. I'm sorry I was such a wet blanket this morning. Like I said, I'm not the best person to give romantic advice right now."

"That's okay. You had a point."

"Maybe. But I still should have kept my mouth closed. Wren always says I speak first, think second, and sometimes don't think at all."

"That's a little harsh."

"Yeah, well, that's my brainy sister for you." Portia pulled out a binder with the printed title *Chocolate Shop Events.*

"Events not event?" Rosie commented.

"Well if this one is a success—and I intend to make certain it is—then don't you think we ought to do more?"

"I like how you think." Rosie went around the counter so they could look at the pages together.

Portia had an index tab for *Dark Magic Chocolate and Wine Event.* Within that section she had copies of her email correspondence with the gentlemen from the wine store.

She flipped a page. "These are the pairings they're suggesting. What do you think about the order?" She pointed to a section she'd highlighted in pink.

Rosie read through carefully. Emerson and Clifford had suggested a California merlot to be paired with Sage's single origin dark chocolate. "I agree this one should be first. Then we can gradually work up to the sweeter chocolates and wines."

"So, we should do the zinfandel next? They've suggested that would complement our dark chocolate dreams truffle."

"Yes. And then the dried cherry and hazelnut dark chocolate bark with the vintage port."

"So, do we finish with the rasteau and the salted milk chocolate caramels? Or the fruity chardonnay with the macadamia nut white chocolate truffles?"

"Gosh. I'm not sure. They're both very sweet. Should we ask Sage her opinion?"

"I don't think so. She made it pretty clear to me that this was our gig. How about we end with the chardonnay and white truffles? The chardonnay should leave a cleaner finish to the palate for the evening."

"Good point. Man, I can't wait to try all these fabulous combinations." And she sure hoped Brant would enjoy them, too. Provided he agreed to go with her.

Portia sighed. "I'll have to do my enjoying vicariously."

Rosie glanced at her friend's still very flat tummy. Of course, being pregnant, Portia would have to abstain. "After the baby's born we'll do a reenactment."

"After the baby's born. You don't know how terrified I feel when you say that."

In Portia's shoes, she'd be scared as well. "Maybe it would help if you talked to your family about it."

"I don't know. I had a phone call from Wren last night. She told me if I didn't go back and finish college I'd basically be ruining my life. I can just imagine how supportive she'd be if I told her I was pregnant."

"Maybe she'd surprise you?"

"I doubt it. I think my mom will be okay—once she gets over the shock. But it might be easier to start with Aunt Sage. She's super sweet. No matter how crazy her kids get, she's always so calm and patient."

"Not Callan?"

Portia shrugged. "I love her, but she's kind of blunt. A bit like Wren. Not sure I want to start with her, either."

"You have another aunt. Dani, isn't it?"

"Yes. I absolutely love her. She was actually my prof for my introduction to Psychology class. If she lived closer, I would probably have told her already."

"But she doesn't, so Sage it is. You should tell her soon. Maybe tonight?"

"Maybe."

In other words, no. But Rosie had already pushed hard enough.

"Guess I should get back to painting my house," Rosie

said, going toward the door.

Outside a woman ran by the window, traveling at quite the pace. A blonde woman, dressed in black pants and a white shirt…

Sara Maria!

Rosie hurried out of the shop and dashed after her. She was soon overtaken by Brant. They ran for over a block, before realizing Sara Maria had too much of a head start on them. Gradually they slowed their pace.

"Wh-what was that a-about?" Rosie huffed, trying to catch her breath. She'd didn't think she'd sprinted that fast since her last track and field event in high school.

Brant looked exasperated. "All I said was—" He stopped, thought a minute, then shook his head ruefully. "I guess I should have been more tactful."

"Oh, no, Brant."

"Look, I was just saying what needed to be said. Her employer needs to know she requires supervision around equipment like gas ranges and ovens."

"Brant, that time you told me she left the oven on and almost started a fire—how old was she?"

He took a few minutes to think. "A teenager, maybe."

There were ten years between them, and Brant had left home at eighteen. "So you were already working and living at Three Bars Ranch?"

"No. I was still at home. So she must have been younger."

"Eight, Brant. If you were still at home, she couldn't have been more than eight. Don't you think it's possible she's matured a bit since then?"

They were half a block from the care home now, but Brant abruptly stopped walking.

"So, you think I'm a jerk of a brother."

"I wouldn't have put it that way. But it this case... yeah."

He crossed his arms over his chest. "I think I've had enough for today."

"Enough *what*?"

"Enough of trying to protect my sister. Enough painting. Enough of..."

She held her breath wondering if he'd say *you*.

"Just enough, okay? I'm going to take off for a while."

And then he did exactly that.

BRANT WAS STEAMING mad for most of the hour drive back to the ranch. He hardly noticed the beauty around him. The golden aspen trees showing off against the blue Montana sky. The geese flocking in perfect formation for their migration south. The silver dustings of snow on the tops of the highest mountain peaks.

It seemed in that moment there was precious little to enjoy in life.

It was so easy for others to judge. They had no clue what

it had been like, growing up as Sara Maria's brother. All the bullies he'd had to fend off for her. All the days and nights he'd had to forgo playing with friends because he had to look out for his kid sister.

His mother had been grateful—but never Sara Maria. She'd always acted like she was putting up with him as much as he was putting up with her.

And Rosie. Every single time an issue came up she took Sara Maria's side over his. One would think after the night they'd spent together she would have been a little more understanding.

Back at the ranch he hunkered down in the bunkhouse, curtly refusing an offer to play poker with the guys. Still, the sound of their laughing and roughhousing kept him up until they finally called it a night at eleven o'clock.

Even in the silence though, he couldn't fall asleep.

Eventually his anger subsided and he was able to see the situation from another angle. Many of his ideas of what his sister could and could not do were based on the past. Sara Maria was eighteen now, and she'd matured, especially since the death of their mother.

While Rosie hadn't had to look after a challenging younger sibling, she had been down a similar road as him, making sacrifices for the sake of someone she loved. How had she managed to give up so many years to look after her parents without turning bitter?

Was hers an example he could maybe learn from?

Once he'd admitted his culpability—and faced up to the atonement he needed to do—Brant finally fell asleep. The next morning he was determined to set matters right, starting with his sister.

He drove straight to the care home and tracked her down.

She was in the far corner of the lounge area, sitting by a window and reading that damn *Kant* book again.

"Hey, sis, I've come to apologize." He dragged one of the chairs closer to her and sat down.

She wouldn't look at him.

"That job is perfect for you and I screwed it up. If I can help set things right, I'll be glad to do it. Want me to go talk to that boss of yours?"

Finally Sara Maria set her book down on her lap. "Yesterday Rosie told me to go back to work. To tell them I could do the job and that I was sorry for running out the way I did."

He reared back a few inches. "And what did your boss say?"

"She said it was fine, but not to run out again if I got angry. She said I need to go to her and tell her how I feel. And I said I would."

"Well, that's good. So you still have the job?" He ought to feel more relieved about that.

After a bit of reflection he realized he'd been looking forward to solving the problem for her. Not very commendable on his part.

"She said I make the best pies she's ever tasted. She said she'd be a fool to lose me because I might go into business for myself and become her competition."

Sara Maria gave a small smile here, and it hit Brant in the gut. She so rarely smiled around him.

"Way to go, sis. I guess there's nothing more for me to do then."

"No."

Brant stood up. He wasn't sure his sister had accepted his apology, but at least he'd made it. Now it was time to face Rosie.

"DAMN THIS PAINT can. It feels like it's been glued shut." Rosie's straight edge screw driver was pried between the can and the lid. Even using all her weight on the lever, she couldn't get the darned lid to budge.

"Let me help you with that."

Her muscles tensed. Slowly, she stood up. Brant was walking across her front lawn. Behind him was his parked truck. Thanks to a neighbor mowing his lawn three doors down, she hadn't heard him drive up.

Her mouth felt dry as she watched him approach. She would have loved to see his eyes but it was a bright, sunny day and he was wearing the sunglasses he used for driving.

Was he still angry with her? She wouldn't blame him if

he was. She'd been awfully blunt, in a situation which really wasn't any of her business. He'd asked her to spend time with his sister—not to become her caregiver.

Still, she didn't regret what she'd said. Even if this was going to be the end of her relationship with Brant, well, that had never been intended as a long-term thing anyway. And if driving some truths home with Brant ended up making Sara Maria's life easier, it would be worth it.

As Brant drew closer, he held out his hand.

At first hope flared—he was reaching out for her. But then she realized he just wanted the screwdriver.

She passed it to him and, of course, the lid popped open as easily as a jar of homemade jam.

Brant stood tall and finally slipped his glasses up on his head. The expression in his mossy green eyes was certainly not angry.

"I'm sorry for yesterday, Rosie. I was out of line."

"Oh, Brant." Relief washed over her. "I had no right to say those things to you."

"Maybe not, but I'm glad you did. I've had this idea of who Sara Maria is and what she's capable of. I've been living with that idea for years. And I'm only now realizing it's way out of date."

"I think she'll be very glad to hear you say that."

A frown line formed between his eyes. "I was just talking to her ten minutes ago. I went to say I was sorry and to offer to try and patch up the situation at work. But she told me you'd spoken to her yesterday. The advice you gave her—it was solid. And it worked. She's still got her job."

"I'm so glad. Being gainfully employed will make her feel useful. And that's important. Especially now that she's eighteen."

"Eighteen. Old enough to vote. Guess I'm going to have to start thinking of my baby sister as an adult."

"If you also treated her like one that would help your relationship a lot."

"Hey, can we hold off on the lectures? I'm still a little bruised from the last one."

"Fair enough." She looked down at the can of aqua paint. "Now do you want to do the front door or should I?"

"You take the door, I'm going to give the window trims one last coat."

"I can't believe we're almost finished."

"By tomorrow for sure. A whole day earlier than I expected. Say, did you talk to Maddie Cash yesterday?"

"She had an unexpected offer come in for another property, so we pushed back our meeting to today. She said she'd drive by the house around noon."

"Okay then, let's get busy. See if we can't impress the hell of her with what a beautiful house this is."

Rosie smiled then picked up her paint brush. Since Brant was working on a different side of the house today, she didn't have his hot body, or conversation, to distract her. By ten minutes to noon, she'd finished the last coat of paint on the front door. She stepped back to the street so she could admire the overall effect, and that was when Maddie drove up.

The realtor, looking stylish in a smart linen pant suit that hugged her figure as if it had been sewn in place, got out of her car.

"Rosie, I love the colors you chose. The ivory and white are timeless. And the aqua door gives the house a touch of pizazz."

"Thank you." Rosie gazed fondly at the home she'd lived in for all of her life.

It had needed this facelift so badly, but now with the fresh, clean paint job, the essential beauty of the place shone through.

As did the memories.

She could recall her mother waiting on the porch for her to come home the first day she was deemed old enough to walk to and from school on her own. In the far corner was the apple tree Daniel had dared her to climb when she was only six. She'd managed to make it to the first bough, and then he'd left her stranded while he went inside and got a popsicle, which he promptly ate in front of her.

It was going to be so hard to leave, when the time finally came.

"I think another open house is definitely in order." Maddie pulled out her phone to check her calendar. "What about this Saturday? Or would Sunday be better?"

"Either date works for me."

"Excellent. We'll make it Sunday. Rosie, I wouldn't be surprised if we had an offer within the week. I'm so excited for you!"

Chapter Sixteen

AT FOUR O'CLOCK Rosie left Brant to put the finishing touches on the trim while she showered and changed, then headed downtown to pick up some steaks, baking potatoes, and greens for a salad. By the time she returned, Brant was folding up his ladder.

"Well, darlin', we're done. What do you think?"

She stood slightly behind him, resting her hands on his shoulders and gazing in admiration at her house. "It's perfect. Thank you so much."

"My pleasure. As for me, I sure appreciate all you've done for Sara Maria."

"Was it a fair deal? I feel like I got the better part of the bargain."

"I assure you, I don't feel cheated in the slightest." He turned then so he could wrap his arm around her. With his other hand he touched her chin, studied her expression, then kissed her.

Rosie suddenly had no interest in steak.

And neither, apparently, did he.

TWO HOURS LATER, however, Rosie was ravenous. She lifted her head from Brant's sculpted chest.

"How does that steak sound now, cowboy?"

His eyes brightened. "Yeah. I forgot about those."

"I'll take that as a compliment." She checked the time on her phone surprised to see it was only six.

They dressed, and then Brant went outside to fire up the barbecue, while she pulled the seasoned steaks from the fridge and prepared the veggies, nuking the potatoes which could then be finished in the barbecue.

When Brant came back inside, he had a bottle of red wine, which he opened and then filled two glasses.

"To your future, Rosie."

Anxiety pinged in her stomach. Living for the day was fine, but only when she never thought about tomorrow. She would have preferred to toast to *their* future.

But she forced a smile. Had a sip of wine and then another. Soon she convinced herself that not until her house actually sold did she need to worry about being separated from Brant.

"Barbecue should be hot now. I'll put on the grub."

She handed him a pair of tongs and the plate with the meat and foil-wrapped potatoes.

While she was setting the table, the house phone rang, reminding her she really ought to cancel the service. Almost all her calls came through her cell phone anyway.

"Hello." She watched through the window as Brant put the food on the grill. He noticed her and winked.

"Rosie, glad you're home. You didn't answer your cell."

It was her brother. "Sorry, I must have left it on mute. What's up?"

"I have big news!"

Rosie moved to the island, turning her back to the window.

Daniel sounded so excited. For a second she wondered if Glenda might be pregnant. But that wasn't it.

"One of the major networks really likes our script. They're optioning it for a TV show, with plans to start shooting in just three months!"

"Wow, Daniel. Wow."

"Right? And there's more."

Rosie sank onto one of the bar stools. "What?"

"I've given them a series overview and they love that, too. They want us to start working on the next episodes."

"Hang on. This sounds serious." Daniel's scripts had been optioned before, only to have production stall for years.

"It is. Listen to the people behind the project." He listed a bunch of names that didn't mean much to Rosie. But when he mentioned the actors being considered for the roles, her eyebrows went up.

"You have to move to L.A. pronto."

"But the house. It still hasn't sold."

"That doesn't matter. Our producers want to meet the

other half of the writing team. There's going to be a big party next week when they announce the actors playing the lead roles. You can't be hiding in the shadows in Montana anymore. It's time you got full credit for the writing you do. And your share of the option check, too."

He mentioned a number that made her gasp. No wonder he wasn't worried if the house sold.

"I only fill in a bit here and there."

"Not true, sis, and you know it. That last scene was almost entirely your writing. And it was brilliant."

"That's nice to hear. I'm glad you thought my contribution was helpful."

"Helpful? Stop being so modest. How soon can you get out here? I'll gladly book you a ticket for tomorrow if you can manage that."

"Gosh, Daniel. I have to give Sage at the chocolate shop at least a week's notice." Though, Sage would understand. She'd been anticipating Rosie's departure for months. And now with Portia on the payroll, Rosie's departure wouldn't be as problematic as it would have been.

Rosie put a hand to the side of her head, which felt like it had begun to spin. What about Sara Maria? *And Brant?*

But this was the opportunity she'd been dreaming of. This was her moment. "I need to talk to some people before I book my flights to L.A. How about I call you in a few days?"

"Okay." Daniel sounded disappointed. "I expected you

to be more excited about this."

"I guess the prospect of change is scarier than I expected. But I am super happy. I mean—wow. A TV series!" As she said goodbye and hung up the phone, Rosie had the eerie sense she wasn't alone in the room.

She turned, and sure enough Brant was standing at the open screen door with a tray of baked potatoes and grilled steak.

BRANT SET THE food on the table. Some key facts were falling into place for him. Little things he'd noticed combined with the snippet of conversation he'd just overheard.

He studied his Rosie. She looked the same with her soft round face, small, full mouth, lovely brown curls. But inside her head there were secrets she'd never told him. Maybe never told anyone.

"I take it that was your brother calling from L.A.?"

"Daniel. Yes." She replaced the phone in its cradle, then paused. Slowly she glanced back at him. "He was calling with news. Maybe you heard?"

"I heard a bit. Sounded like he sold one of his scripts and it's going to be a TV show?"

Rosie filled in the details of the deal for him, but he couldn't quite take it all in. The part he was really interested in—the part that involved Rosie—still hadn't been mentioned.

"So. This opportunity. It sounds fantastic."

"It's big. Like winning the lottery for a screenwriter."

"And how is this going to affect you?" *Us?*

"Daniel wants me involved in the project. If he had his way, I'd be on a plane tomorrow."

Brant sucked in his breath. "That soon?"

"I told him it wasn't possible. I want to give Sage a week's notice." She tilted her head and gave him a sad smile. "This move has been my dream for so long. But I never imagined it happening this fast."

He took a few steps toward her and before he knew it, she was running to him, as well, throwing her arms around him and pressing her face to his chest. He wrapped her in his arms and rested his cheek on the top of her head.

"Tell me something, Rosie?"

He could feel her muscles tense.

"Sure."

"The other day, when I took a shower in your dad's bedroom, I noticed some papers on his desk and I took a look. I'd never seen a script before, but I could tell that was what this was. I assumed you'd printed out something your brother had written, and I never mentioned it to you because I was kind of embarrassed about snooping."

Rosie pulled back so she could look at him. "Want me to tell you the whole story?"

"I think I already know. You wrote those pages, didn't you?"

"Yes. Yes, I did."

"How long have you been a writer?"

"I loved writing stories when I was a kid, but I dropped the habit once my Mom got sick. I didn't start again until three years ago. Daniel was home for Christmas and he asked if I would proofread a few scenes. Soon he was vetting all his work through me, and eventually I began making a few changes here and there. Daniel especially liked the way I wrote dialogue and... well, slowly my contributions grew larger."

"That's impressive."

She shrugged. "It didn't seem like much to me at the time. But this pilot we just finished... I wrote most of the dialogue. The story concept was Daniel's though, as was most of the plot and scene progression. Turns out we make a great team."

Brant thought fleetingly of his own sister. The two of them had never made a great team. If they tried to work on a project together, they'd both end up crazy.

"So you're a cowriter, then."

"I never felt that way on the other projects I helped him with. I didn't feel my input was that significant."

"But this time..."

"This time, yeah. I feel I wrote close to fifty percent of the final script. Daniel's insisting I get my share of the credit and financial reward."

"And he's right."

"I suppose so." She broke out with a smile. "I mean, yes. I actually wrote the entire last scene of the episode entirely myself."

"Well then, we should be celebrating." Brant tried to inject some enthusiasm in his voice as he retrieved their wine glasses and made another toast. "To your new career in L.A."

They clinked glasses and sipped wine. The liquid seemed to curdle in his gut, but he forced a smile all the same.

DINNER WAS COLD when they finally sat down to eat, but it didn't matter because their appetites had cooled, too. Brant watched Rosie mash her baked potato until it was practically paste.

"Too excited to eat?"

"Yes. But also nervous… and sad."

"This is your dream. Your big opportunity. You should be happy." He tried to sound upbeat, for her sake.

"Think of all I'm leaving though. The chocolate shop and my friends. This house. Huck. Sara Maria." She let out a long, wavering sigh. "And you."

"Goodbyes are always tough. But all those things you mention will still be here. You'll be able to visit."

But would she though? Once she acclimatized to her new life in L.A.?

He doubted it.

They cleaned the kitchen together without talking much.

When they were finished the silence became awkward.

"You work tomorrow, right?"

She nodded.

"So you'll give Sage your notice?"

"I suppose so. Yes."

"Which means you'll be flying out next Friday?"

She paused to think. "Yes. I guess that's right."

"I'll drive you to the airport."

"I wouldn't want to—"

"I'll drive you to the airport. No arguing, woman."

"No ar-arguing." As her voice caught on a sob, he reached for her and held her tight.

He could have stayed the night. He had a feeling she wanted him to. But he had a lot of thinking to do.

Besides, if he was going to have to learn to live without her, he figured he'd better start getting used to it.

Chapter Seventeen

AFTER LEAVING ROSIE'S, Brant didn't head to the ranch at first. Instead he drove to the May Bell Care Home and parked on the opposite side of the road. Counting windows, he figured out which room was his sister's. In the entire building, she was the only resident who still had their light on at eight-thirty in the evening.

Brant groaned. Rosie and the care home staff were right. He had to spring his sister from this joint.

But that wasn't the only change he needed to make with his life. He needed a job—something with a future, not an annual contract working as a wrangler on another man's ranch. He'd always dreamed that one day he'd buy his own land and livestock. But he had no way near enough money to do that.

So where did that leave him?

He thought of Rosie and the way she'd smiled at him that morning after he'd apologized. It was hard to believe that smile—and the woman who went with it—were going to be out of his life soon.

Brant swallowed hard. Pressed his fist against his forehead.

Memories from the day his mother died came back to him. She'd called him the week earlier and explained she had to go for some medical tests. Could he take a day off work and stay with Sara Maria.

He hadn't asked what the tests were for and it turned out it didn't matter. Because on her way back to Marietta a deer had run across the highway. The truck ahead of her hit it first, then his mother's car rammed into the truck going full speed.

Somehow the driver of the truck had survived. The deer—and his mother—hadn't been so lucky.

It sucked how life could change in an instant like that. All it took sometimes was a deer running across a road… or an unexpected phone call just as he was about to sit down for dinner.

Eventually Brant drove back to the ranch, but he slept poorly in the bunkhouse. He tried not to think about Rosie. She was going to be fine. More than fine. Probably one day he was going to see her on the Academy Awards or something.

Meanwhile he had his own life to worry about. And his sister's. He still had a day left in his vacation. And come morning he realized what he needed to do with it.

First he placed a phone call, arranged a time for a meeting, then got back into his truck.

Jem Miller was just wrapping up a meeting with an architect when Brant arrived at the Miller Barns Construction office building at ten o'clock. Jem ran his business on the same acreage where he lived, midway between Bozeman and Marietta. He had a huge workshop in a converted old, red barn and his offices were above that in what would have once been the loft.

Brant had been impressed with the man when he'd helped him put up the horse barn on Three Bars Ranch. Seeing his operation up close like this, Brant knew if he couldn't spend the rest of his life working his dream job on his own ranch... this might come a close second.

Brant sat on the edge of his chair during his entire forty-minute meeting with Jem Miller. He explained that he wasn't just here to offer casual labor. He wanted to be a carpenter. He wanted to specialize in horse barns, like Jem.

Jem was one of the best in his field and one day Brant intended to join those ranks.

"Son, I'll admit I was impressed with how fast you learned when you were helping me at Proctor's. I made up my mind then that if you ever came knocking on my door, I'd give you a job. That's why I left you my calling card when the barn was complete."

Brant felt as if a load of bricks had been removed from his chest. "I hoped that was the case, Mr. Miller. But I didn't want to presume anything."

Together they discussed the terms of the job. Jem named

a salary that was a little less than what Brant made now. But after a period of apprenticeship he'd soon be making a lot more.

The men shook hands and Brant left feeling a hell of a lot better than he had on the way in. Letting go of his dream of owning his own spread was hard. But he had to be practical. A career at Miller Barns would be fulfilling and he'd be doing the right thing by his sister at the same time.

As he drove back to the Triple Bar, to give his notice, the sense of satisfaction he'd been feeling slowly ebbed away and he found himself thinking of Rosie again.

The depths of the misery he felt about her imminent departure surprised him. Neither of them had gone into the relationship with much in terms of expectations. And he hadn't been seeing her that long.

None of that added up to how terrible he felt at the prospect of losing her.

When the truth hit him, he almost swerved off the road.

He was in love.

It had never happened to him before, so maybe that was why he hadn't realized it until this morning. But only love could explain why he hurt so badly.

And wasn't it just his luck to fall for a woman he couldn't have.

ROSIE SHOWED UP at work the next day with the nervous

feeling she used to get before exams. She didn't need to broach the subject of her resignation with Sage, though, because her boss read the news the instant she saw her face. Portia was in the kitchen, too, packaging the molded chocolates Sage had made a few days ago.

"What's up Rosie? Something happened, I can tell," Sage said. "Did you sell your house?"

"No but I had a call from my brother." Rosie explained about the TV pilot, her hand in helping to write it, and her brother's insistence she fly to L.A. as soon as possible.

"A TV series? That's incredible Rosie. Congratulations!" Sage gave her a hug, and so did Portia.

"You seriously write screenplays?" Portia looked impressed and amazed. "That's what you were doing when I saw you typing away on your laptop?"

"I started out small, helping Daniel with the odd bit of dialogue. But I wrote the entire final scene of the episode that's going to be our TV pilot."

"Good for you, Rosie. That's amazing," Sage said.

"You *have* to invite me to L.A. for the premier, or whatever they do for TV pilots," Portia said. "Oh, I can't believe this is happening. It's so wonderful!"

Yes. On one level Rosie agreed. But she couldn't quite work up the enthusiasm she knew she'd have felt a month ago, before she got to know Brant.

"When are you planning to leave?" Sage asked.

"I want to give you fair notice, of course. Is a week

enough time? I was thinking next Friday would be my last day."

"That's fine," Sage said.

"Good." Rosie smiled, but inside she didn't feel good at all. There was something rather sad about knowing she could be so quickly and easily replaced.

"Oh, my gosh," Portia said. "What about the chocolate and wine pairing night?"

"I know. I hate to miss it. But my brother is really anxious for me to get to L.A." She would leave her tickets with Brant when he picked her up to take her to the airport. She hoped she would see him before then, but she didn't dare count on it. She hadn't heard a word from him since he'd left last night. Not a phone call, not a text message.

Obviously he considered their relationship over.

Yet, he'd insisted on driving her to the airport. But maybe that was a courtesy thing?

For the rest of that day, whenever there was a lull in business Portia hit her with questions. She wanted to know everything about the story, about how Rosie started writing, and about her brother and his life in L.A.

By the end of the day Rosie had a headache—and she never got headaches. To her credit Portia finally picked up on her ambivalent feelings.

"I'm sorry, Rosie. I've been so excited about your news. But it's hard for you, right? I know what it's like to live your entire life in one place and then have to go somewhere new. I was so afraid of leaving home for college. And of course for you there's Brant to consider. You two were off to a great start and now this."

Yes. Now this.

"I'd be a fool to let this opportunity pass me by. But it's weird. It's like I've spent so many years dreaming about a new, exciting life, and now that it's right in front of me—I can't remember why I wanted it."

"You're just nervous. At least you'll be going to live with family. I bet you'll adjust faster than you think."

At the end of the day, after Portia had left to drive to the Circle C, Rosie flipped over the "Closed" sign. Then she went back to the deserted kitchen, which was sparkling clean, just the way Sage had left it when she went home hours ago.

Rosie tossed her apron into the laundry basket. Then she pulled out her phone and dialed Brant.

He sounded out of breath when he answered. "Hey, Rosie, what's up?"

She had hoped for something a little... sweeter. But she couldn't back out now. "I need to tell your sister I'm leaving next Friday. What's the best way to do it?"

"I've been worrying about that, too. She hates change, and even though you've only been in her life a short while, she might get really upset."

"Yeah." Unlike Brant, who seemed to be just fine with the idea.

"How about we tell her together? I can be at the care home in about thirty minutes. Want to meet me there?"

He couldn't be at the ranch if he was going to meet her in Marietta in thirty minutes. But since he hadn't volunteered any information about where he was, Rosie didn't ask.

"Sure. See you then."

ROSIE WENT HOME to feed Huck and to grab a quick bite of dinner before heading to the May Bell Care Home. As she left her home she had to stop and stare at it. It would take a while to get used to the new look.

Brant's truck was already parked on the street across from the home, and he hopped out of the cab when he saw her.

His smile was warm when he looked at her, but he didn't reach for her. Or kiss her.

"How did Sage and Portia react when they heard your news?"

She sighed. "They were thrilled. My last day is Friday. My brother's already booked my flight for nine o'clock that evening."

"What time should I pick you up?"

"How about six at the chocolate shop?"

"Sure."

She gave him a look of exasperation. Did he have to sound so darned cheerful about this? "You seem happy."

"Happy would be a stretch. I'm making changes in my life, too, Rosie. I just gave my notice at Three Bars Ranch. In two weeks I'm going to start apprenticing as a carpenter at Miller Barns."

She had a hard time processing this. "You're going to build horse barns?"

"Yup." He didn't look very excited.

"But I thought you loved working as a ranch hand."

"That life style is fine for a young guy. But I've got responsibilities. This job at Miller Barns will offer regular hours and make it possible for me to find a place in Marietta where I can make a home for my sister."

"Wow. I had no idea you were contemplating such a big change."

"I didn't either. People have been telling me for a while now that the May Bell Care Home wasn't right for my sister. Just this morning it hit me what I needed to do."

She was impressed with the maturity and thoughtfulness behind his decision. But she also felt sad for him, that he was giving up a lifestyle he loved to take care of his sister. She would have asked more questions, but Brant was holding the door open for her, and inside Sara Maria was waiting for them.

Brant's sister looked pleased at this unscheduled visit, but also curious. "I got your text message Brant, saying you were coming to visit. But it's Thursday."

Rosie's heart ached a little to hear that. What must it be

like to only have visitors on a regimented basis? It must make Sara Maria feel like she was an obligation, a chore.

When she thought of the news she was about to impart, Rosie felt even worse.

"Let's talk outside." Brant suggested. "It's so nice out."

Sara Maria and Rosie settled on a vacant bench to the left of the main doors, while Brant remained standing. He took a wide-legged stance, resting his weight back on his heels.

"We have some news," he said getting straight to the point.

Sara Maria's face tightened with anxiety. "Is it good news?"

Brant sighed. "You remember Rosie is planning to move to Los Angeles to live with her brother one day?"

Sara Maria's eyes widened. "It's not happening soon, is it?"

Rosie reached for her hand and squeezed the cold fingers. "I'm afraid so. My brother needs my help on an important project. I'll be leaving next Friday."

"No. No. *No.*" Brant's sister withdrew her hand and pulled it in close to her body. She shook her head violently and her face went pale.

"We can still talk. I'll come back for visits," Rosie said, desperately trying to reach the younger woman.

But it was clear Sara Maria couldn't hear her. She'd withdrawn inside herself, tucking up her legs and covering her ears with her hands, all the while chanting that one word over and over. "No. No. No…"

From the beginning, Rosie had dreaded having to deal with one of Sara Maria's meltdowns. And now it seemed it was finally happening. She tried to touch the other woman, but Sara Maria recoiled with such force that she upended herself onto the lawn, with her back against the metal bench legs.

She was moaning now, the sound like nothing Rosie had ever heard before.

In desperation Rosie turned to Brant, who was fixed in the same spot, hands fisted, jaw clenched, apparently petrified.

If his sister was being attacked by a grizzly bear, Rosie had no doubt Brant would leap forward to protect her. But these fits of Sara Maria's, these psychological breakdowns, they rendered him helpless.

She had to take charge.

"Brant, go tell the staff what's happening. I'll stay with Sara Maria and make sure she doesn't hurt herself."

To her amazement, Brant didn't take off running. Instead her words seemed to have galvanized him. He blinked, and then stepped around her.

"No, I'll stay with my sister. I can handle this."

BRANT'S EARLIEST MEMORIES of his little sister were of a sweet, smiling baby. As soon as she learned to crawl, she would follow him everywhere in the house, and he played endless games with her, willing to do almost anything to hear her infectious, gurgling laughter.

As a toddler, she'd been precocious, always getting into his stuff and interfering when he had friends over. He hadn't minded much. She was still so darned cute.

Shortly after her second birthday, though, all that changed. Almost overnight Sara Maria transformed from a chatty, curious being, to a silent, unresponsive one. Neither Brant nor his mom could get her to smile anymore, let alone laugh.

And Brant would never forget her first no-holds-barred fit. It happened in the grocery store when the sales clerk offered her a sticker. She went crazy, crying and whimpering and covering her ears with her hands in a characteristic maneuver that Brant would come to know extremely well.

Brant was scared by these changes. And he was hurt. Why didn't his little sister love him anymore?

More and more he avoided being around her. Mom was the only one who could handle her, anyway. When Mom died, he'd turned to others to solve the problem of Sara Maria. The staff at the care home. Rosie.

But the care home wasn't the answer and Rosie was leaving.

So what was going to happen to his sister? Watching her moaning on the ground he fought the urge to turn his back and leave. Instead he tried imagining what was going on inside her head. She had to be suffering terribly to be acting this way.

Somewhere inside this adult-looking, eighteen-year-old was the sweet little baby sister he'd once adored. Shouldn't he be doing something to try to help her? Even if he had no clue what that was?

All these thoughts raced inside Brant's head in a matter of seconds. He felt like he'd been in some sort of trance, then when Rosie called his name, when she told him to go for help, he suddenly snapped out of it.

He heard himself tell Rosie that he would deal with this. And then he sat on the grass beside his sister, using his body as a barricade so she wouldn't bump her head against the metal legs of the bench.

She turtled into a tighter ball, arms cushioning her head as if she wanted to block out the world.

Brant fought his own discomfort, instead trying to focus on what she was feeling.

"I'm sorry. I know Rosie has been a good friend to you. And losing her is going to hurt. That probably scares you." It sure as hell scared him when he thought about it, which was why he did his best not to think about it.

Surprisingly Sara Maria grew quieter. Still in her protective ball she murmured. "Rosie is my only friend."

"That's not true. You've got me." He let out a derisive snort. "I know I'm not much. In fact, I've pretty much sucked as a brother for a long time. But things are going to be different."

Sara Maria was listening, he could tell.

Since the onslaught of her autistic symptoms, Sara Maria hadn't tolerated any sort of physical contact from him. Yet he remembered Mom hugging her. She must miss it. Didn't everyone need some sort of human contact?

Pushing aside his fear of being rejected, Brant wrapped first one arm, then the other, around his sister. As he held her close, he pictured the little one-year-old smile, heard again her mischievous laughter.

His sister surprised him again when she didn't pull away. Instead he could feel her muscles relax.

"I can't make the sort of home for you that Mom did. But I am going to do my best. I've got a new job, one closer to Marietta, and I'm going to buy us a house. You'll get to leave the care home. Keep your job at the bakery."

Quiet fell as Sara Maria absorbed his words. "I would like that. But why does Rosie have to leave?"

"She has a special talent as a writer. She and her brother have a chance to have their stories turned into a TV show that millions could watch. This is such a big deal for her. We have to make it easier for her to leave us. Not harder."

"I don't want to let her leave."

"But you have to think about what Rosie wants."

Sara Maria let out a long sigh. Then something else occurred to her. "What about Huck?"

He laughed. "Yeah, I forgot about that old dog. I know

Rosie can't take him with her. Maybe she'll let us adopt him."

A shudder of delight passed through Sara Maria's body. "Ohhhh, really? I would love that."

"And Huck would love it, too," Rosie said.

Startled by her voice, Brant glanced up. Donna was beside her, so clearly Rosie had gone inside to ask for help. How long they'd been standing here he had no idea.

"Are we really going to all live in the same house? You, me, and Huck?"

He didn't give his word often, and his sister knew it. "I promise."

Then the unthinkable happened. His sister gave him a big hug. Over his sister's head, he saw Rosie watching with tears in her eyes.

He quickly glanced away. "No need to get all emotional on me." But even as he said the words, he hugged his sister tighter.

Chapter Eighteen

A S SHE LEFT Brant to talk about his future plans with his sister, Rosie realized that her path to L.A. had just become clearer. She didn't need to feel guilty about Sara Maria—Brant would take care of her. For whatever reason he'd finally moved past his block. He'd managed to be empathetic, to really listen, and to be there when his sister needed him.

Furthermore, she could now leave Huck in good conscience, knowing he would be taken care of and well-loved besides.

It was as if the fates were conspiring to get her to L.A.—and to separate her from Brant.

As glad as she'd been to see him connect with his sister, a big part of her wished it was Brant, not Sara Maria, who didn't want to let her go. Maybe she wouldn't want to see him fall apart the way Sara Maria had. But he could at least have the decency to be sad.

Rosie kicked through a clump of aspen leaves on the sidewalk, already transitioned from gold to brown, reminding her how quickly time was passing. She had just six days to pack up her stuff, and to make arrangements for leaving her house.

At some point she and Daniel would need to return to do a final clear out of their parents' possessions and furniture. Oh, how she dreaded that day.

Throughout the rest of the evening, Rosie kept checking her phone but Brant didn't call or leave her a message. On Friday, Rosie went to work already anticipating the end of the day when Brant would come by for his box of salted chocolate caramels.

Portia was off for the day, so Rosie was alone in the front while Sage prepared a batch of champagne truffles in the kitchen. News of her eminent departure had already spread and a few of her regular customers wished her well and told her they would miss her.

At quarter to noon, Sage emerged from the kitchen to say goodbye. "I've volunteered to be a parent helper for Savannah's classroom trip to the abandoned copper mine, so I have to be going. Did you sell any more tickets for our event?"

"Two, bringing us to a total of twenty-two—" Not counting herself and Brant, who would not be going after all. "I wish we had more space. I'm sure we could easily sell more than the twenty-six we have room for."

"That's what Portia said, as well. If this event is as successful as it sounds like it will be, I'm going to talk to Stanley

Scranton about leasing more space. The travel agency has been gone for over a year. The only problem is, Stanley's such a crotchety, old guy. He'll think I'm expanding because I'm making a ton of money and he'll try to gouge me on the rent."

"Still, it can't hurt to ask, right?"

Despite a steady flow of customers—and the sale of four more tickets to their event—the afternoon dragged. An hour early, at four-thirty, Rosie was already watching the street for signs of Brant's long, broad shouldered frame, his purposeful stride, the white cowboy hat that shielded his expression so well.

But he didn't show.

At quarter to five, Krista Martin from Blue Sky Advertising dropped in to see if she could help publicize the upcoming chocolate and wine tasting event. Since the event was practically sold out already, Rosie put her off. Krista was from New York and her big city glamor was a little intimidating. But she took one of Krista's cards for Sage and Portia in case they decided to use her services in the future. Before she left Krista ordered a hot chocolate to go.

"This stuff is totally addicting."

"Sure is." Rosie blinked back a tear. Starting Sunday she would have to give up her daily Copper Mountain Chocolate treats. It wouldn't be easy.

At five-thirty-one it occurred to Rosie for the first time that Brant might not come at all.

A customer in a hurry breezed in at quarter to six and Rosie helped him select some assorted truffles for his wife for their wedding anniversary. Normally she would have chatted with the man, asked him what flavors his wife enjoyed most. Today though she just grabbed random truffles, boxed them up and sent him on his way.

After that she pretty much stared out the window watching couples stroll by with their arms linked, mothers and fathers with their children. It seemed no one in Marietta was alone this Friday night except her.

Finally it was six. Closing time. She scrolled through her phone looking for missed calls, text messages, an email. But all she found were two messages from her brother and one from her sister-in-law including a picture of the gorgeous casita that was waiting for her.

"You've also got your own private patio if you get sick of hanging out with Daniel and me. Can't wait to see you! xoxo Glenda"

Not a word from Brant explaining why, after three and a half months of regular patronage, he wasn't buying a box of chocolates for his sister today.

For a man who lived in fear of disrupting his sister's schedule, it didn't make sense. Unless something bad had happened to Sara Maria. His sister had seemed okay when Rosie left them last night. But maybe she'd had another breakdown later in the evening? Once she had the idea, Rosie couldn't stop worrying. She decided to call the care home and check.

The receptionist on duty, however, assured her Sara Maria was fine.

"She and her brother are watching TV in her room right now. Would you like me to transfer your call?"

"No, no, that's fine." Phone still in hand, Rosie sank to the floor.

The pain began in her stomach, and then grew hotter and sharper. It seemed Brant was spending his Friday, as usual, with his sister. Not only had he not invited her to join them, but he'd wanted to avoid her so badly he hadn't even purchased his sister her usual chocolate treat.

She wasn't even gone and he'd already written her out of his life.

She shouldn't care so much. Ahead of her lay adventure, possibly fame and fortune, too. But her heart and her body ached only for Brant.

Eventually Rosie picked herself up from the floor. Slowly, like someone who had been very sick and now needed to move with extreme care, she went through the steps of closing the shop for the day.

On her walk home, she chose a roundabout route that offered no possibility of encountering Brant and Sara Maria as they made their way to the Pizza Parlor. At home she went directly to her parents' bedroom and sank down beside Huck.

"He told me from the start he lives for the moment. I guess he's moved on to the next moment."

Huck lifted his head and stared at her with his sad, butterscotch-colored eyes. Then he gave her hand a lick, as if to say *"I know how you feel."*

"When I'm in L.A., I'll be too busy to even think of him. And I'm sure I'm going to love living with Daniel and Glenda. My room looks gorgeous. Plus, this will give me a chance to really get to know my brother—we haven't lived in the same zip code, let alone house, since I was eight."

Huck licked her hand again. It was as if he was really listening to her.

She was going to miss the old boy.

And with that thought, the weight of all her losses became too much for her to bear and she started to cry.

Rosie spent Saturday preparing for the open house the next day. In the morning, she decluttered, getting rid of old magazines, knickknacks, and everyday objects that somehow hadn't been returned to where they belonged. She took three boxes of old clothing and household items to Goodwill, a bag of magazines to recycling, and two bags of trash to the dump.

In the afternoon she cleaned, making sure the sinks and plumbing fixtures sparkled, and placed lavender-scented sachets in all the closets so they would smell sweet and fresh when prospective purchasers checked out the storage space.

For dinner she ate a bowl of cereal and then rewarded herself by watching old episodes of *Grey's Anatomy*. Oh, how she loved the season premiere for that show. It was exciting—and terrifying—to imagine that one day her TV series might be available on Netflix.

Sunday morning Rosie baked apple cinnamon muffins using Portia's recipe. The delicious aroma still lingered, as she'd hoped it would, when Maddie came by at eleven to host the open house.

"The difference in this place is amazing," she gushed, as she set out a sign-up sheet near the front entry. "I'm feeling really psyched. Today might be the day, Rosie!"

"I hope so," Rosie said. But did she?

When she thought about this house passing on to a strange new family, she actually felt sick inside.

"What's that delicious smell?"

"I did some baking this morning. The muffins are in a basket in the kitchen. Please help yourself."

"Isn't that sweet. Thank you, Rosie." Maddie moved around the living room, plumping the pillows, and then adjusting the window treatments so they let in the most flattering amount of light. When she was finished, she surveyed the room with a satisfied smile, until her gaze landed on Rosie.

"It's best if you take Huck and leave. Buyers feel uncomfortable if the owner of the house is hovering."

"Don't worry. We'll be going soon."

Rosie had already made a plan that would get her out of the way of the open house and hopefully take her mind off all the craziness of the past few days. She grabbed her backpack and Huck's leash, and then whistled to the lab.

She walked the path to the trailhead for the waterfall hike. While the air had a cold bite today, the sky was clear— perfect hiking weather. She hoped to channel the many times she'd done this trail with her family, but instead she kept picturing Sara Maria and Brant. She recalled almost word-for-word everything she and Brant had talked about that day.

At the waterfall, she sank onto picnic rock and recalled the way he had looked at her, and how she'd felt when he touched her hair, as if she was melting from the inside out.

She and Huck returned to the house at three-forty-five, fifteen minutes before the open house was scheduled to end. They entered quietly from the kitchen. Rosie filled Huck's food bowl, noticed most of the muffins were gone, and then followed the sound of voices to the family room.

To her surprise, Brant and Maddie were engaged in an animated conversation. They fell silent when they spotted her.

"You're back!" Maddie said brightly.

Rosie said nothing, just studied Brant, trying to read his expression. Had he dropped by to see her, after days of silence?

His impersonal smile told her nothing.

"How are you doing Rosie? You must be busy getting ready for the big move."

His words were as dispassionate as his smile. It was as if they were two acquaintances, not a man and a woman who had been lovers four days ago.

"Good news, Rosie," Maddie continued after a brief pause. "We've got a buyer who's really interested."

"That's great," Rosie finally managed to say.

Maddie looked puzzled by her flat tone. "Yes, it is. I'm heading to the office to draw up the paperwork. Is it okay if I call you later tonight with the official offer?"

"Yes, of course. Thank you for everything."

When Brant accompanied them to the front door, Rosie was afraid he might slip away with Maddie. But he lingered on the front porch, waiting until the realtor had driven away to say, "You don't seem excited about the offer."

She tried to catch his evasive gaze. "Just tell me this. Is the offer coming from you?"

Chapter Nineteen

B RANT HAD HOPED to be gone before Rosie came home. He was trying so hard to do the honorable thing—to leave her free to follow her dream. But seeing her in person was a test of his resolve he didn't know if he could pass.

She'd obviously spent the day outside—her skin glowed and she had the smell of trees and fresh air about her. He wanted so much to touch her. To stop himself, he gripped the porch railing hard and glanced out at the street instead of into her eyes.

"Do you care who buys your house? Isn't the point to get your money and cut your ties so you're free to go?"

"Should I take that as a yes?"

He gave a short, rueful laugh. He should have known he wouldn't shake her off the topic easily.

"I'm putting in an offer, yes. I don't have a realtor so Maddie's handling the paperwork for me."

She said nothing for a while, then in a puzzled tone, "But why?"

"I'm making changes in my life—a lot of them are well

overdue. I told you about the new job. Next I need to buy a house. Sara Maria is desperate to get out of that damn care home. And now that she's got a job she needs to be in walking distance of the bakery."

"Okay, but there are other homes for sale in Marietta that meet those qualifications."

"Maybe. I've grown attached to this one."

Too attached, in fact. It worried him some that living here would make it that much harder to get over Rosie. But if he didn't buy this house, she might use it as an excuse not to move to L.A. And he couldn't let that happen.

Rosie did so much for other people. She'd spent years helping her folks, and in the few weeks she'd known them, she'd done so much for him and his sister. It was time Rosie did something just for herself.

She herself had said a chance to write for a major new TV series was like winning the lottery. It didn't happen to many people and, when it did, it changed their life. If Rosie let this opportunity pass, she would surely regret it.

BRANT'S STORY DIDN'T add up. Rosie believed the part about him needing to buy a house. But he was glossing over his reasons for buying *hers*.

"Have you looked at other houses on the market?"

"Why would I, when this one is perfect?"

"Purchasing a house is a major deal. You don't just put

in an offer for the first one that catches your eye."

"Turns out I do."

He still wouldn't look at her and there had to be a reason. What was he afraid she would see in his eyes? She went to stand beside him. Noticed his knuckles were turning white he was gripping the railing so hard.

She touched his arm. "Brant?"

"I have to go."

She tightened her hold on him. "Why would you avoid me all week and then turn around and buy my house?"

"I didn't avoid you. I was just... busy."

"Too busy to send me the occasional text message? Or to buy your sister's chocolates? You can't tell me Sara Maria suddenly lost her taste for salted chocolate caramels."

"It just seemed..." His shoulders rose as he sucked in a deep breath. "It was too hard to see you, Rosie. I'm trying to do the right thing here. Make it easy for you to go."

"And you think breaking my heart makes it easy for me?"

Finally he let go of the porch railing. Slowly he turned his tortured gaze to her. "Don't say that. You haven't known me long enough to say that."

In a moment of clarity, she understood and a huge weight fell of her chest. He hadn't been acting out of indifference, but unselfishness motivated from a deep sense of caring. Maybe even love.

She stared into his eyes and saw the hungry way he looked at her.

"My sweet Rosie. Stop torturing me."

"If you mean for me to stop looking at you like I love you, then I'm sorry, but it simply isn't possible." She hoped he could see in her eyes exactly what she saw in his.

Love.

Her attempt at telepathy obviously worked because he groaned, and then he was cupping her face and kissing her. Lips first, then her cheeks, her nose, the tip of her chin.

"You're so addictive. Why didn't you warn me?"

She had to laugh. "Back when you were my five-thirty cowboy, I didn't think I had a chance with you."

"It was me who never stood a chance. Ah, Rosie, what am I going to do without you?"

She wrapped her arms around him, holding him tight. The words they'd just exchanged—they changed everything, didn't they? She pressed her face to his chest where she could hear his pounding heart. "I don't want to leave you."

He stroked her back the way a parent might soothe a child. "You feel that way now. But I won't let you stay. Seriously, Rosie. You have to move to L.A. There is no other option."

"But—"

"I have to go now, Rosie. I've instructed Maddie to put in my offer at your asking price. So when she comes to you later tonight, just sign the papers, okay? If you can't do it for yourself, then do it for me."

NEWS TRAVELLED FAST that Rosie's house had been sold. On Monday, Portia, Dakota, and Sage took her out for dinner at the fancy Graff Hotel to celebrate. Rosie noticed Portia ate very small portions of her smoked rib and coleslaw dinner. Sage seemed to be keeping a close eye on her niece as well. Later, when just Portia and Rosie were in the washroom, Rosie asked if Portia had told her aunt about the baby.

"I did. She was super nice and sympathetic."

"That sounds like Sage."

"Trouble is she wants me to tell my mom."

"You're going to have to eventually."

Portia sighed. "Don't I know it. But it won't be easy at all. Aunt Sage didn't press me with questions about the father. Mom won't let me off so easily."

Rosie wished she knew why Portia was so reluctant to talk about the dad, however the last thing she would do was pry. "I wish I wasn't leaving you to handle all this alone."

"We'll stay in touch. And there's always Facebook and Instagram. You have to post lots of pictures from L.A. Promise?"

"I will, but it won't be the same."

"I feel the same way. These past few weeks have been some of the hardest of my life. I don't know how I would have managed without you. You were so kind and support-ive. Rosie, I'm going to miss you so much."

They hugged and Rosie was touched when she saw tears glimmer in Portia's eyes.

On Wednesday, Sara Maria came to Rosie's house with a sour cherry pie, decorated with a cut-out heart in the center.

Rosie invited her in. "I know you don't like pie, but I have some salted chocolate caramels. Would you like some of those?"

"Oh, yes."

They sat at the kitchen table and Rosie put out a candy bowl with a variety of Sage's chocolates. Then she cut a slice of the pie, scattering flakes of buttery pastry over the old oak table.

After her first taste, she sighed. "This is so delicious. If anything, you're only getting better."

"Brant says I'm not supposed to say that I wish you weren't leaving. But I am allowed to say that I'll miss you."

"I'll miss you, too." Rosie didn't dare say more. Too much sadness was welling up inside of her. There had been so many goodbyes this week. And the hardest one was yet to come.

On Friday, Rosie went to work with her bags packed, ready to drive straight to the Bozeman airport after closing. Tears filled her eyes as she gave Huck one last hug. Though the sale of the house wouldn't close for another thirty days Brant and his sister would be moving in this afternoon.

They'd agreed she would leave the furniture and all the kitchen stuff. But Rosie had cleaned everything out of the bedrooms. Anything she wasn't taking with her was stored in boxes for when she and Daniel came back to do the final move.

By the time she made it to work, Rosie's eyes were dry, but she knew that wouldn't last. All day long old friends, neighbors, and customers made a special point of stopping in to wish her well.

At quarter after five, she freshened her lipstick, even though she wasn't expecting Brant to show up until six. But at precisely five-thirty she spotted his familiar form out the front window. He strode up to the door, removed his hat, and then stepped inside.

Joy and sorrow rose up inside her. She struggled to keep her voice from trembling. "Good afternoon. May I help you?"

Without taking his eyes off her, he moved up to the counter. "I'd like a box of chocolates please."

"Any particular kind?"

Eyes twinkling and fighting a smile he said, "I hear those cocoa peanut melts are good."

She did a double take. "The cocoa peanut melts?"

"Yeah. I'll take four of those. And then maybe some of the champagne truffles?"

Slowly he worked his way through all of the chocolates she'd recommended to him over the months he'd been shopping here. When the box was full, he asked her to wrap it up nicely.

"Your sister must be broadening her horizons," Rosie said when she handed over the copper box with its festoon of curly ribbon.

"These aren't for Sara Maria. Now that she's got a job I figure she can buy her own chocolates."

"And how does she feel about that?"

"Actually I think she enjoys having her own purchasing power, and the freedom that goes with that. At Donna's suggestion, I took her to a new doctor this week and he feels that as long as she's in familiar territory, she ought to be fine walking to work and running errands in town. He's also recommended a therapist who's going to work with her on coping strategies to deal with anxiety and stress."

On the drive to the airport Brant talked a bit about his hopes for his new job, and Rosie shared the latest details on the chocolate and wine pairing event. She put the tickets she'd purchased in Brant's glove compartment and told him he should still go—and take a friend, too, if he wanted.

"I'll think about it," he said.

No sooner were they out of sight of Marietta than Rosie began missing her dog, Sage and Portia, Sara Maria and her home.

She couldn't imagine what was waiting for her in L.A. Daniel and Glenda were so excited for her arrival, but she felt only nerves.

At every highway exit she prayed Brant would turn his truck around and take her home. She wanted him to tell her he loved her and that he couldn't let her go.

But before she knew it they were pulling up to the departures level of the Bozeman Yellowstone International Airport.

"Want me to park and help you carry your luggage inside?"

"No. Just drop me off." If their farewell was prolonged by another minute, Rosie was certain she'd start bawling.

And then everything happened quickly. No sooner had Brant pulled up to the curb and unloaded her two big suitcases onto a cart, than an airport porter came by to hurry them along. At the same moment a big SUV pulled up behind Brant's truck and the driver tapped on his horn.

"I guess this is it." Brant reached into the cab and pulled out the box of chocolates.

"For me?"

"Who else. I figured it might take you a while to find a new chocolate source in L.A."

She tucked the box in her carry-on, trying not to sob. He was making this sound so final and she couldn't handle that.

"I'll be back... one day."

He gave her a sad smile. "Sure. I know."

She longed to hurl herself at him. But the porter was hovering and the driver of the SUV was hunched over his steering wheel and glowering.

Brant stooped and gave her a chaste kiss. "Good luck, Rosie."

She could not say goodbye. She couldn't say anything. She stood, clutching the handle of the luggage rack and watched as he drove away, feeling more bereft and alone than she ever had in her life.

Once his truck was a speck, she swallowed back a sob, and then straightened her shoulders. Goodbye, Montana. Hello, L.A.

Chapter Twenty

October 31, Two weeks later

ROSIE SENSED THE moment Brant entered the Copper Mountain Chocolate shop. Slowly she turned toward the door and in the room filled with twenty-six guests all in costume, instantly spotted him.

He'd come dressed as a vampire, in an elegant, dark dinner jacket, with his curly hair slicked back and his handsome face pale under a sheen of makeup. His eyes felt like lasers as they homed in on her, following her every movement as she weaved through the crowd toward him.

He didn't kiss her, but his gaze intimately drank in every detail of her appearance.

She was dressed as a witch in a black gown that skimmed her curves, then flared out from her knees and continued down to the floor. Her hair was wild and curly and she'd sprayed it with sparkles that matched the vibrant purple, gold, and silver makeup around her eyes.

He took both of her hands and seemed to study every inch of her. "You look... bewitching."

"Do I?" She was the one who felt spellbound.

She couldn't tear her gaze from him. She'd only ever seen him in jeans, but with his height, broad shoulders, and narrow hips, he totally owned his elegant evening apparel.

The vampire makeup and hair gave him just the right touch of a spooky edge to make her genuinely shiver.

Or maybe she was reacting to the touch of his hands.

She was so, so glad to see him again.

"I didn't expect you to be here," he said.

"I wasn't sure, myself, until last night." When she'd finally made the booking she'd asked Portia to pick her up at the airport, and they'd gone to Sage's house to prep for the event.

They were all going as witches in a variety of elegant black dresses. Sage's was long and flowing like a caftan, while Portia's was mid-thigh length, and coupled with long, sleek black boots. Sage had hired a talented makeup artist to paint their faces and she'd done such a good job that from a distance it seemed like they were all wearing masks around their eyes.

"I decided I couldn't miss this."

"The store looks great."

The lights were dim. Silver lights sparkled from the ceiling and golden candles flickered on each of the tables. Display cases had been pushed back to accommodate six bar-height tables which Sage had rented for the event.

"Good evening, everyone." Sage was standing at the table

nearest the kitchen, flanked by the owners of the wine store—Emerson in a Dumbledore costume and Clifford as Professor Snape. "Welcome to our dark magic chocolate and wine pairing evening."

"We're hoping to tantalize your taste buds with some exquisite chocolate and vintage spirits tonight," Emerson continued. "You'll find menus on all the tables, along with pens. We encourage you to make notes about your impressions and any special likes and dislikes."

"Very handy for placing your chocolate and wine orders at the end of the evening," Clifford added with a saucy wink.

"Our first tasting will be of Copper Mountain's single origin, dark chocolate along with a California merlot."

Dakota and Portia emerged from the kitchen, bearing trays of chocolates and wine glasses. As they distributed them to the guests, Sage first talked about her chocolate, and then Emerson and Clifford elaborated on the wine.

Brant picked up a square of the dark chocolate, and then surprised Rosie by bringing it up to her lips. Delicately, she took a taste, closing her eyes to savor the rich, intense flavors, first a touch of cinnamon and hazelnut, followed by a sweeter, almost caramel note.

When she opened her eyes, Brant was watching her. Without breaking eye contact he took his own taste of the chocolate. The intimacy of the experience was incredibly arousing and, with the dim lighting, it was possible to imagine they were the only two people in the room.

Next Brant passed her the wine glass and she sipped the merlot, allowing the flavor to explode in her mouth, melding with the bittersweet aftertaste of the chocolate.

She had to give credit to the guys from the Two Old Goats wine shop. The combination of flavors was terrific.

For the next course, Rosie took the initiative, bringing the dark chocolate dreams truffle to Brant's lips. He opened his mouth slowly, his gaze dark with intent as he slowly cut through the creamy chocolate. She let the tips of her fingers linger by his mouth, and then slowly pulled away.

"Now the zinfandel." She passed him the glass and watched as he swirled the wine in his mouth.

The evening evolved in a leisurely pace, with plenty of time between courses for making notes and visiting with the other guests in attendance. Rosie felt she ought to mingle, but she wanted only to be with Brant.

Slowly they progressed from the dried cherry and hazelnut dark chocolate bark, to the salted milk chocolate caramels and finally to the macadamia nut white chocolate truffles.

Sage and the guys from the Two Old Goats wine store had some parting words, then encouraged guests to stay and mingle—and possibly place orders for some of their favorites from the evening menu.

A handful of guests chose to leave at that point, but the majority lingered.

Brant and Rosie found themselves alone at their table.

"You haven't talked much about L.A.," Brant said.

"It was incredible. Daniel introduced me to his agent—who is now my agent by the way—and to the executives at the network. We sat in on some of the auditions and I actually met Rachel McAdams."

"Was she glamorous?"

"She was actually really friendly. The parties were sure glamorous though. Glenda took me to her hair dresser and to her manicurist." She held out her hands with their silver gel nail polish "We also went shopping and I bought two evening dresses and some very strappy sandals."

"I bet you looked amazing."

"Maybe you'll come to a party with me sometime and find out."

"An L.A. party? I don't think so."

"Why not? You might find them more fun than you expect. I sure did."

"Good," he said, though his eyes looked pained. "I'm glad to hear it. So the L.A. life is just as exciting as you expected?"

"It's wild and crazy and I guess a few weeks a year will be more than enough for me."

"Rosie... what are you saying?"

"Daniel and I have done a lot of talking. I finally convinced him I can write from anywhere. And I can Skype in on the meetings. So there's really no need for me to actually live in L.A. if I don't want to."

She paused. Swallowed. "Assuming you want me here, that is."

When she lifted her gaze, Brant was watching her. Without breaking eye contact he cupped her face between his hands. "I want you here. Very much."

And then he touched his lips to hers. All the chocolate and wine tastings had been a mere prelude to this, what she had hungered for the most—his kisses and his arms around her.

"Let's step outside for a minute," Brant said, his mouth next to her ear.

Taking his hand, she led him out the back way. With his arm around her to keep her warm, he led her down Main Street to River Bend Park. It was late now—all the little trick-and-treaters were safely at home. Brant avoided a group of teenagers hanging out behind the courthouse, and led her to a bench by the library.

"I love you, Rosie, but I don't want me—or my sister—to ever be a drag on your career."

"I've been given a great opportunity but, after just ten days in L.A., I already know it's not the right place for me. I love you, Brant, and Marietta will always feel like home. My career will probably have ups and downs, and involve travel from time to time. But I know I will always want to come home to you."

To her amazement he pulled a ring from the breast pocket of his dinner jacket.

"You had this planned? All evening I've been so nervous, and you were intending to propose?"

"I couldn't stop hoping, Rosie. I figured if you showed up, my chances would be good."

"Since the first day you walked into the chocolate shop, your chances have been good."

Brant slipped the ring on her finger. "Then I've sure wasted a hell of a lot of time."

She laughed. When she'd planned this event with Portia all those weeks ago, she'd never guessed that she and Brant would be the best pairing of the evening. She could hardly wait to tell their family and friends the good news.

But tomorrow would be soon enough for that...

The End

Don't miss the next book in...

The Love at the Chocolate Shop series

Book 1: *Melt My Heart, Cowboy* by C.J. Carmichael
Book 2: *A Thankful Heart* by Melissa McClone
Book 3: *Montana Secret Santa* by Debra Salonen
Book 4: *The Chocolate Cure* by Roxanne Snopek

The rest of the Love at the Chocolate Shop is coming soon!

The Carrigans of Circle C

Hawksley Carrigan, owner of the Circle C Ranch south of Marietta, Montana, always wanted a son to carry on the family name. Unfortunately for him, he ended up with four daughters.

Book 1: Promise Me, Cowboy
Book 2: Good Together
Book 3: Close to Her Heart
Book 4: Snowbound in Montana
Book 5: A Cowgirl's Christmas
Book 6: A Bramble House Christmas

Available now at your favorite online retailer!

About the Author

USA Today Bestselling author C. J. Carmichael has written over fifty novels in her favorite genres of romance and mystery. Three of her novels, *The Fourth Child*, *Perfect Partners* and *A Bramble House Christmas* have been nominated for the *Romance Writers of America* RITA Award. When not writing C. J. enjoys family time with her grown daughters and her husband, including hiking in the Rocky Mountains around their home in Calgary, and relaxing at their cottage on Flathead Lake, Montana.

Visit C.J.'s website at CJCarmichael.com

Thank you for reading

Melt My Heart, Cowboy

If you enjoyed this book, you can find more from all our great authors at TulePublishing.com, or from your favorite online retailer.

TULE
PUBLISHING

Made in the USA
Las Vegas, NV
01 June 2023

72832857R00150